A DAY IN THE DEATH OF WALTER ZAWISLAK: A LOVE STORY

MOLLY O'KEEFE

To Adam, who gave me this idea. To Robert Zawislak, dear family friend and science teacher extraordinaire - thank you for the use of your name. To the editors and writer friends who have helped make this story grow beyond what I thought I could make it. Particularly Jude.

To Katy Dockrill for this perfect cover.

Cam Drynan for your beautiful work on the audiobook.

And to you reader! Thank you so much for coming along with me on this journey. I can't tell you how much it means to me.

A DAY IN THE DEATH OF WALTER ZAWISLAK

If, at the end of your life, you got to pick one day to relive, what day would you pick?

Walter Zawislak wants none of it. Not a day to relive, not a trip down memory lane through a life he wasted. His wife, Rosie, died twenty years ago, and without her he hasn't done much living. So if it's lights out for him, then just turn them off already and let him get some peace and quiet.

But Peter, the mysterious young man in charge of Walter's afterlife, isn't listening to Walter. In Peter's eyes there is beauty in every day, even the bad ones. Even the really bad ones. Of which Water has had more than a few. But there are also days of bravery and heroism. Selflessness and grace.

And Rosie...there are lots of days of Rosie.

Before it's too late for both of them, Peter has to remind Walter that there's more to life than dying.

W alter had no idea where he was going, but he kept on, shuffling down the long gray hallway like a good soldier.

"Hello?" His voice echoed back without reply. Customer service at St. Mike's was slipping, if you asked him.

Used to be you couldn't even sneeze without a dozen nurses coming in to take your blood pressure.

He guessed he was walking from his room, one of the cheap ward ones where he and the rest of the guys on Medicaid were pooled, but he couldn't be sure. The drugs they'd kept him on since he was admitted were disorienting. The other night he could have sworn Matt Saunders, his next-door neighbor who died two winters ago, came into his room to fight about that ladder Walter borrowed and broke.

This isn't the cardiac wing. Walter was sure of that, at least. That wing had yellow and green walls, soothing colors so as to not create any undue excitement for weak tickers.

Watercolor pictures, like the ones in the cardiac wing, hung on the walls, except these landscapes and pictures of cottages and birds were the color of slate and thunder-clouds. Gray everywhere.

Strangest damn decor he'd ever seen.

He blinked and rubbed his runny eyes, but nothing changed. Last round of blood thinners must have screwed up his vision. His right leg throbbed, from deep inside where the scar tissue originated, out through bone and sinew like chain lightning.

Where the heck did I leave my cane?

Suddenly, he was aware of a high-pitched ringing in his ears. A steady squeal. He stopped walking to dig into his left ear, where it seemed to be loudest, but it didn't help.

Must be coming from behind one of them gray doors. Someone's heart monitor with bad news.

Good thing he had his slippers and that he had remembered his robe. The other day, he woke up to find a woman standing over his bed. He had been startled, or rather figured he should be startled, but the drugs took the edge off most things and when she had turned around he could see her whole dimpled backside.

Since then he had insisted on wearing his robe at all times.

He put a hand to his heart, startled by the ease with which things were working in his chest. The constant tightness he'd long grown used to was missing. He took a deep breath, filling the low and withered bottom third of his lungs that had been neglected since the last heart attack.

I must be getting discharged. For once he was going to leave the hospital healthier than when he went in. A miracle.

"Hello? Anybody home?" He knocked on one of the gray doors but not a soul answered him or poked their head out to see what the ruckus was. There must have been trouble someplace, Walter guessed. All the doctors and nurses must be working on someone behind a different gray door.

He became increasingly weary. His feet started to drag, and the rasp and swish of the rubber soles on the linoleum accompanied him down the long hallway. He squinted again, his attention caught by the blurry shape of something green up ahead.

The green blur eventually gained the form of a tree, a healthy and radiant ficus in a gray pot. So green it seemed to glow like the LCD readout on his bedside clock. Beside the tree was an empty chair and Walter sat down with a grateful moan.

Better or not, he needed a rest.

Tucking his tingling hands into the pockets of his old terry cloth robe, he noticed that what had previously been dark blue with orange–pink bleach spots had turned gray.

He blinked. Hard. But it stayed gray.

I'm gonna have to ask the doctor about my eyes.

"Sorry I wasn't here to greet you."

Walter jumped at the sound of another voice and turned to find a slight young man with light brown skin fumbling with an armful of files.

"You're early," the young man said.

"I'm sorry, but I don't really know—"

"Of course not, because you're early and I wasn't here to greet you." The man's smile was razor thin and Walter got the impression things had gone wrong because he was early.

The guy looked to be about twenty—though Walter had long since lost his ability to guess a young person's age with any accuracy. He always guessed ten years younger. Everyone looked like a pup.

This pup was dressed in black. What in the world had

happened here at St. Mike's? They never used to have gray walls and doctors never dressed in black.

The place was going all new-agey.

Can't say as I like it.

"Do you hear that?" Walter dug into his left ear. The ringing was making him crazy. "That ringing?"

"You're going to be difficult aren't you?"

"I'm not trying to be."

"Of course not. None of you ever do." The boy sighed heavily and tapped a button on his fancy phone.

Miraculously, the buzzing stopped.

"That's a good trick." Walter smiled, trying to be amiable, hoping it would get him out of here sooner.

"If you would follow me?" The boy gestured to the open door behind him.

Walter shuffled after him into the small gray office and sat in a chair across from a cluttered desk. The back wall was a big window through which Walter gazed out at the brightest blue sky he had ever seen. The brilliant blue was dotted with cotton-ball clouds, as his daughter used to call them. Clouds so fluffy and white they seemed false.

Cotton-ball clouds. He hadn't thought of that in years.

"Looks like a good day." Walter squinted at the light.

"It usually is." The boy sat, pulling himself up tight against his desk. "Let's see what we've got here..." He paged through a few more files. "You'll have to excuse me, the holidays are always a busy time. I'm sort of swamped."

"What holiday?"

The boy looked up at him with dark, nearly black eyes. "Christmas, Hanukkah, Los Posadas, Winter Solstice, the New Year."

"You've got to be kidding me."

"As a rule, no."

"But I was admitted just after Thanksgiving." Walter could have sworn only a few nights had passed.

The boy pulled out a file. "Here you are. Walter Zawislak, December 28, 2012."

"That's the date?"

"Yep."

"Today's date?"

"I think I've established that I don't joke, Mr. Zawislak."

"It's just...a coincidence, that's all."

"I'm afraid I don't know what you're talking about." The boy flipped open the file and Walter pondered the coincidence of being released from the hospital on the same day his wife died twenty years earlier.

"I just need to make a few changes here. We weren't expecting you for another two days." He pulled a pen from his shirt pocket and hit the top with his thumb. "We're still trying to iron out some of the communication problems from head office."

Walter couldn't care less about communication problems and knew nothing about head office so he watched the clouds form and break behind the boy's head. Twenty years. That made him sixty-six years old. Rosie would have been seventy and Jennifer was thirty-eight. Those years between Rosie's death and this day stood like a wall. A dividing line. Now and Then. Before and After.

"Now." The boy handed him some paperwork, and his irises, Walter noticed, were now blue, the color of the sky behind him. Never seen a person with eyes like that. Must have been a trick of the lighting, or Walter's old runny eyes.

Where did I leave my damn glasses?

"If you have any questions after we're done talking then you can just refer to the FAQ sheet."

Walter nodded because the boy seemed to expect it.

"We've had some changes in policy here due to over-crowding. People linger indefinitely because they can't stand to leave. They feel they don't have..." The boy twirled his hand in the air and the clouds outside the window behind him all spun apart at that moment. Strange. "...closure. Peace."

"I just want to go home," Walter said, hoping the boy would cut his little discharge speech short. He knew the one at St. Mike's by heart. "Wanting to leave is not a problem."

"Right. That's why we've changed the policy."

"You're saying the policy is that I can't go home?"

"No, the policy is changed because you want to go home and can't."

"Why can't I go home?"

The boy stared at Walter for a long time and Walter, never comfortable with scrutiny, looked down at his robe and was relieved to see that it was blue again. But out of the corner of his eye the boy seemed to grow younger and lose a little of his shape, as if the outline of his face was feathering out, blurring. Walter blinked and looked back at him head-on and the boy's features solidified.

"I'm sorry. I am a bit out of sorts from your arrival." The boy rubbed his forehead. "Let me start again."

"Please do." Walter wished he had a watch. There was the mail and the lawn. He needed to get some flowers and head over to the cemetery. He wasn't sure where his car was and he—

"You've crossed over."

Walter blinked. The boy blinked back.

"Say again."

"You've passed away. Died."

2

Between them sat an odd moment of silence in which Walter could actually hear the blood in his veins. He flexed his fingers and the tingles continued. His stomach growled. He had to take a leak. Physical realities for a living person. He was no more dead than he was a bird.

"That's not very funny."

"I don't joke." The boy smiled, a small nervous flutter of a smile, that hit Walter like a kick in the gut.

"What the hell are you talking about? Is this the psych ward?" He bumped the desk when he stood, sending files into the little shit's lap.

"Please, sir, sit down and I swear I will make this clear."

Walter sat, mostly because he was lightheaded.

"People always have a hard time with the news, which is why we've changed the policy."

"The discharge policy?" He must have been taken to a different hospital, that fancy one in Milwaukee. "This isn't St. Mike's, is it?"

"No, Walter, this is not St. Mike's."

Walter nodded and swallowed. He felt the mechanics of his throat, the solid lump of worry and fear that refused to be swallowed.

I'm not dead. This was another one of those dreams. Damn drugs.

He felt foolish for having been worried. A dream would explain the gray walls and this half-baked kid. He relaxed back in his seat.

"In the previous millennium, people could linger here after dying and watch their funerals. Watch their children grow and their spouses grieve. Most of the time, the soul gets tired of watching these things and moves on—"

"On? On to where?"

"I am aware you are no great believer, but let's not be obtuse."

"You're talking about Heaven?"

"And Hell."

Walter grunted. Usually his dreams weren't so damn philosophical. He swiveled in his seat hoping Dan Saunders might stumble in to talk about that ladder.

"In any case..." The boy leaned back, putting his hands behind his head, and Walter thought he could see the blue of the sky through his black shirt. Like it was see-through, except he couldn't see the kid's arms. The whole thing was a little transparent.

"We've always had some stragglers, people who have hung around to see what happens on Earth. Conspiracy theorists and religious fanatics mostly, but the numbers have grown. Times have gotten increasingly more difficult— heart disease, obesity, diabetes, murder, war, school shootings. People are taken from their lives before they are ready and thus don't have peace with leaving their families, their loved ones. So they stick around and we can't accommodate everyone anymore."

"Kick 'em out."

The boy scowled at him, which reminded him of the puppy he'd gotten Jennifer for her seventh birthday, a fierce little thing despite its size and overgrown paws and ears.

"It doesn't work that way," the boy said. "Instead, we have come up with a plan to help people gain closure and move on. Everyone has to do this. Without exception."

The boy paused dramatically and then, as if there had been a drum roll only he could hear, he announced: "You get to relive one day."

Walter's stomach turned. Maybe he'd eaten something that didn't agree with him. That chicken thing with all the sauce was probably at the root of this.

He pressed a hand to his chest and burped. But felt no better.

"Honestly, Walter," the boy said.

"Pardon me?"

"One whole day...most people are quite thrilled with the opportunity."

"Guess it depends on the day." There were plenty of days he'd tried to forget.

"That's the beauty of the new system. You get to pick." The boy held out a page to Walter. "I have selected a list of dates for you, including the highlights that our studies have shown are most popular. Wedding days, birth of children—"

"I missed Jennifer's. I was in Omaha at a conference..."

"Right. Well, then...big promotions at work..."

"I didn't get mine." Walter looked down at the list of dates that he couldn't place in his memory and ignored that slick run of shame down his spine. "I was put in the warehouse."

"These things do happen," the boy told him, and Walter wanted to ask *to whom*? Obviously to him, but Walter was ready to bet that he had pissed away his big moments better than most.

"Which is why..." The boy beamed like a circuit breaker had been flicked on inside him. Walter felt the hair on his arms lift with charged static electricity. "...I've taken the liberty of adding a few. Sadly, people have tried to go back to the day of their own birth, but we find that only complicates things for the mother. All that awareness in a newborn's eyes tends to lead to hysterics. And frankly, some things need to remain a mystery. But you will get a chance to sample from the dates I have selected for you before choosing which of these days to relive. It's a highlight package, one of our finest."

Walter stood, shoving the paper back into the boy's hands.

He didn't want to talk about this. He didn't want any dream to lead him backward to reopen old wounds. He had to wake up in the morning and deal with the ghosts this dream had let out. Relive a day? Not in a million years.

"I've had enough. I want out."

"That's not possible."

Ignoring the cream-sauce-induced apparition, he closed his eyes and imagined himself in his hospital bed, imagined the nubby scratch of the sheets and the steady beep of the monitors. He felt himself surrounded by the warm stuffiness of his hospital room, the smell of overcooked green beans, and disinfectant that didn't quite overcome the odor of illness and fear. He created the backward spiral toward sleep and then opened his eyes, expecting to see the light of the hallway under the door creating shadows in his hospital room.

Instead, the kid was staring at him, wincing. "You're not dreaming."

"I want off these drugs." Walter pushed up the arm of his bathrobe to rip out IV tubes to stop the pumping of whatever hallucinogenic they had him on, but his arms were unscathed. Empty of open sores or old wounds.

"You aren't on drugs anymore. There's no more pain for you. No more heart attacks."

"I want to go back to my room."

"You can't."

"The hell I can't." Walter wrenched open the door and staggered into the hallway. Trick mirrors must have been set up, because all he could see up and down the hall were mirrored reflections of himself stepping out into the bleak passageway.

"What the...?" He swayed on his feet, and the millions of reflections did the same. He lifted his hand and the mirrored manifestations did the same. Bile welled up in the back of his throat and he closed his eyes, shutting out the mirrors. The inevitability he felt creeping up on his blindside.

Dead? Dear God.

"Mr. Zawislak." Walter felt the boy's soft touch on his elbow but he didn't open his eyes in fear that he would get sick. "You've died. You are dead. There's no hospital room to go back to."

"Where's my body? If I'm dead why can I feel everything? My heart is beating and I can breathe, full breaths. I haven't been able to do that in years. And my fingers. I can feel my fingers and my toes aren't..." He trailed off, abruptly mindful of what all that might mean.

"Where are my glasses?" he yelled. "I can't see anything!" His poor vision was the only concrete thing he could seem to keep in his brain, everything else was moving too fast, was too fantastic to believe.

"Your eyesight will correct itself in time."

"Where's my body?"

"I imagine it's still in the room. You haven't been dead long."

You haven't been dead long, what a ridiculous thing to say to a man who had to take a leak.

"Show me."

"Your body?" The boy shook his head. "I'm afraid that's not allowed."

"I don't care what's allowed. If I'm dead, show me the body. I want to see my body. Show me I'm dead. Prove it."

The boy pulled his phone out of his pocket and read whatever it was telling him. "Okay. Fine! Apparently it's okay." The boy watched him warily. "But you have to calm down. You can't go in there like this. You'll only get more upset."

Walter couldn't imagine being more worked up, more distressed. His heart fired too fast and his bowels shook.

The boy grabbed the file on the desk. "Are you sure you want to do this? It's your body. Dead and cold on a bed. It's not pretty."

Walter nodded, because speech in the wild cataract of feeling had deserted him.

3

The room was dark and it took him a moment to find himself in his body. He'd been in that bright room, the clouds, the pup—that had been just a second ago. He didn't walk down any gray hallway or pass the nurses' station.

A blink and he was here, standing in the shadows of his hospital room.

The air was ripe with the pungency of hospital-grade cleaning solution and beneath that, a fecund, sickly odor.

If I'm dead why can I smell this?

"I'm warning you, Mr. Zawislak," the boy scolded from somewhere behind him. "If you begin to get too emotional we can leave as fast as we got here."

Walter wasn't listening.

He spotted the gleam of his glasses on the bedside table and leaned over to grab them.

"There we go—" he murmured as the world became clear again. He turned and found himself looking down at his own face, a death mask against a flat white pillow.

"Oh my God." He fell back against the IV, sending it

rolling across the floor, unfettered by the tubes that had been attached to him. "Oh my sweet Jesus, what kind of dream is this?"

"Mr. Zawislak, this is what you wanted. This was your idea." The boy shrugged. "I wanted to go to your daughter's sixth birthday but you insisted..."

Transfixed, Walter couldn't look away from the gray, gaunt face marked with brilliant red scabs from the nose tubes. This man, this body in the bed looked like him, but a version he had never imagined. Ghostly and monstrous and pathetic all at the same time. Thin white scruff covered his cheeks, the bones of his skull pressed against his skin as if trying to get out.

It was him, and he was old and withered and dead.

It's true. It's real. His heart thudded and thumped and he could hear it, feel it in his brain and in his belly. The boy, the odor of death...all of it receded, faded away into the white noise of the inconsequential.

He had seen dead bodies in the war, bloated and bloodied, covered in flies and horror. But this... Walter reached out a finger to touch the waxy white hand lying so still on the top of the sheet. His flesh, his dead flesh, was cold and dry.

He jerked his shaking hand back.

When had he gotten so old? The sickness and loneliness had cost him, taken from him more than he had ever realized. When had the picture he had of himself in his head become so different from this walking skeleton?

Walter, trembling and confused, stood and ran a hand over his cheeks and jaw, felt the flesh and fat of health, of too many of Rosie's casseroles. He felt like he had thirty years ago, not like the man on the bed who had survived on coffee and packaged egg whites and fake bacon.

And suddenly, like a door banging open, he was *glad* it was over. Sixty-six years and most of it filled with boredom and drink and an anger that embarrassed him now. Done. A life he had tied himself to with routine and habit. Daily efforts to forget the face of his daughter. Monthly trips to a cold grave that had made him feel forsaken and angry. Taking pills. Watching the news. A burger and iced tea on Sunday at Rudy's. Fighting, every moment, the desire for scotch and bourbon, hell, a light beer would have felt like salvation. Oatmeal in the morning. Soup from a can at night. Tinkering with the old lawn mower so the boy from down the street could use it to butcher his lawn. Wake up. Go to bed. All of it so that he could die alone in a bed at St. Mike's.

He laughed, once. A dry and brittle and rusty noise from his gut. "Well," he said. "You're right. I'm dead."

He turned to the boy whose back was to the door. "I appreciate you bringing me here. What..." He laughed again, this one looser, lighter. He was filled with an ease, a welcome lightness, as he cast off what remained of his humanness. "What happens next?"

"Well, let's go over this list—" The boy pulled his fancy contraption out of his pocket and studied it while the door behind him opened. A nurse walked in, standing in the bright yellow slice of light that was cut out of the dark room. Her face folded into sad, resigned lines.

"He passed away forty minutes ago," the woman said to someone obscured by the door. "I am so sorry for your loss."

"We should go," the boy said, but Walter shot him a quelling look.

Someone was coming to see his dead body. He wanted to know who. Mark? From over at Rudy's. Maybe Rudy? Rudy might get off his fat ass to come and see him. Lord knows he'd spent enough money there over the years to warrant a deathbed visit. And Walter's brother, according to the last Christmas card he received, was still alive. Maybe The Prince had come to see him dead and buried.

The door pushed open further and the light changed the room, creating dark corners, a radiant pool of golden light and a lot of gray space that was the same color as the hallway he'd been in.

A woman walked in. Small and petite with long curly hair touched with fire from the hallway light. She unwound a scarf from her neck and mumbled a thank-you to the nurse.

Something tugged at Walter, a breathless disbelief.

The woman turned and the light fell across her face. A beautiful face. Lined and serious and flushed from cold or tears. A face remarkably similar to her mother's.

Walter clapped a hand to his mouth and his eyes burned with sudden hot and painful emotion.

"Jennifer," he breathed.

"Take as long as you need," the nurse whispered and squeezed Jennifer's shoulder. The nurse couldn't see Jennifer's face crumple in soundless pain but Walter stood right in front of her. And his daughter's silent shuddering meltdown knifed him.

"Thank you," Jennifer said, obviously attempting a normal voice, and the nurse was gone and the room was once again cast into shadows. Agitation rolled off his daughter in waves so palpable even her dead father could feel it.

"Walter?" The boy's voice was disembodied in the darkness. "Remember, it's not good for the recently deceased to get too worked up. Takes everything longer to process."

Walter didn't listen. When Jennifer turned on the

bedside lamp Walter was right beside her. When the tears began to roll off her chin onto his dead fingers, Walter's hands twitched, his arms and body and skin spasmed with the desperate need to touch her.

"Jenny," he groaned. "Jenny, what are you doing here?"

He couldn't take in all the changes the years had made. He had last seen her twenty years ago—a stone pillar of rage and blame. The woman who stood before him, tears dripping off her chin, was beautiful, delicate and fragile around the edges, like gold rubbed thin.

"Jennifer?" The boy appeared at Walter's shoulder, holding his elaborate phone. He tapped at the screen with his finger. "This is your daughter?" His voice was a high squeak.

Walter nodded, his gaze never leaving her as she stood shaking and sobbing over his dead body.

"Listen, you have to come with me." The boy put his hands on Walter's shoulder. "You're too new, it's all too fluid. It's going to hurt. You're not ready—"

Walter felt an odd chasm open up beneath him. Or was it in him? There was a draw on his body, a suck and flush, a dizzying rip, and he sprang loose from this place and time and fell, or thought he fell, backward and the day—that day —the day Jennifer left lay waiting to catch him.

~

MAY 11, 1992
   The Zawislak Home
   314 North Main Street
   Beaverton, Wisconsin

. . .

WALTER JERKED AWAKE, disoriented and sick. *What happened?* His stomach did a slimy twist. *Where am I?* He groaned and put his head in his hands. The rough, worn fabric of his recliner centered him. He'd fallen asleep in his chair. Again.

There was another knock at the door and Walter stumbled to his feet, tripping over a dirty plate and the bottle of bourbon he kept handy for those occasions when nothing but Old Grand-Dad would do.

And those occasions had been one long stretch of nights. He couldn't remember the last time he hadn't rocked himself to sleep with help from that bottle.

"Hold on," he croaked. "Just a second." He tucked in his shirt, a waft of his own sour stink rising up from his body. He slicked back the greasy, unwashed hair dangling into his eyes.

Gotta look good for visitors.

He almost laughed.

Hoping it wasn't going to be Abby from the church, he eased open the door. She had come last week and he'd made promises of attendance he had no intention of keeping. Rosie had been the churchgoer, not him. Rosie had yearned for some sort of peaceful afterlife. He just wanted some peace in the here and now.

"Abby, if this is about church…"

His daughter stood on the step. It was raining.

Both were a surprise.

"Hey, Dad," Jennifer said after a long silence. Raindrops spangled her hair, like diamonds or stars in a night sky.

"Why'd you knock?"

She looked down at her hands, fisted and white-knuckled in front of her. "I don't know."

He did. He knew. The place seemed like a stranger's

house to him, too. And he lived here. He stepped aside and she walked in, and Walter wished he were a little more drunk so that he wouldn't burn with embarrassment at the current state of his housekeeping and hygiene.

"I wish you'd let me know you were coming." He ran a hand over his shirt again, the thin smear of his hair.

"It smells in here, Dad."

"I...ah...I was just going to..." Her gaze, blue and direct like Rosie's, dissected him and he shut up, even hung his head like a guilty dog.

"I've been calling." She shrugged out of her raincoat.

"Phone's broke."

The phone sat on the little table Rosie bought a million years ago at the church bazaar. It didn't work because the old phone was in pieces.

He had smashed it after a brief but fiery conversation with a bill collector. But when was that? Yesterday? A month ago?

"I was getting worried," she said.

There was nothing he could say to that. Not to this woman. This daughter who was like a foreign language. Without Rosie as a translator, he couldn't understand her silences, couldn't read the look in her eye and the tone of her voice.

Her teenage years had been a minefield for him; he'd never known which misstep would send their home into explosions and firefights. He had been gone a lot, on the road, and each trip back it had seemed like a different creature greeted him. Never the little girl he remembered. Instead, a woman with a woman's silences and hidden self. At some point, he'd just stopped trying. He let Rosie navigate their daughter's troubled waters and he handed out the cash.

She went early to college—seventeen. She got a music scholarship and hightailed it out of Beaverton. And he missed her. His baby. The sweet seven-year-old she'd been. Rosie's daughter.

"You hungry?" he asked. "I don't have much, but we could go down to Rudy's—"

"The bar?"

"They've got burgers. We could ask him to do up a tuna melt. You used to love—"

"Dad, Mom's been gone for almost six months." She ran a hand across the dining room table and grimaced at the dust. Dust and clutter had affronted Rosie, and she'd waged weekly campaigns against shoes left by the door and dirty laundry hung over bedroom furniture.

The way he lived now would have sent her into a rage of cleaning.

"Have you gone back to work?"

"I'm on a leave of absence," he lied. He was MIA.

"What about the promotion? Uncle Al—"

"Al said he would hold it. Don't worry about me." He tried to laugh, to divert her attention to some other place, away from the regional director's job that had been given to Ike Broom three weeks ago. That life, his old one, was like a half-forgotten daydream.

Was that him, a salesman? A man with a briefcase and shined-up shoes? His brother-in-law, Al, used to tell him that he had a knack with people. A way with words. Impossible. He was a professional nursemaid, surely. A silent screamer. A drinker. A man paid for his rage and regret with more rage and regret.

It was a full-time occupation being a widower.

"Have you been to a meeting? Have you talked to Barry?"

Walter almost laughed. He was too drunk half the time

to drive to the AA meetings. And since all he would get from Barry, his sponsor, was a speech about how this, too, would pass, he didn't even bother to call. He couldn't take it, not from a man who'd divorced his wife and cursed her behind her back instead of watching someone lower her coffin into the ground.

This, too, was *not* going to pass. Ever.

In the end he couldn't answer his daughter and that was answer enough.

"What have you been doing?" she finally asked, her tone sharp.

"Umm...well, mostly packing up her clothes and putting things in order." The truth was just so glaringly obvious that even he, drunk and rotting, could see it.

A lie seemed in order. *Just the thing.*

Jennifer turned and headed for their bedroom, through the kitchen and up the stairs. Walter followed, stumbling into a chair and knocking the stacks of sympathy cards and junk mail off the table.

Rosie's clothes covered the bed, unpacked. He had tried, but the clothes still carried her scent and the vague shape of her body in the elbows of sweaters and knees of pants. Her dirty socks, lifeless and pale on the floor, still looked like her feet and he couldn't do it. Couldn't box them up to give to strangers. Jennifer scowled and Walter felt a scowl build in him. A headache and an anger.

"You've been drinking." Her voice was icy, but her fingers traced the lace edge of one of Rosie's slips. It was a pale blue one with blond lace that she'd bought before she got sick. "How long since you've eaten anything?"

"I eat."

"You're lying."

Well, there wasn't much to say about that.

"What would Mom say?" she whispered, and his blood went still.

"She's dead."

Jennifer laughed. "Right. I was there, Dad." She was angry and the unsaid thing between them hovered at the ends of their tongues.

I'm sorry, he thought, and if he could have screamed it, he would have. But it wouldn't have done any good. There were too many things to be sorry for. Too many people who needed amends.

The back of his head ached and he thought about that bourbon by his chair.

"She would hate that you were drinking again."

"She's dead." His words and vision were sloppy.

God, he wanted a drink. Needed a drink. Jennifer didn't understand, had never understood. He'd always failed in her eyes, even when she was young. Nothing about him pleased her.

Damn you, he thought and hated himself. Hated her. Hated Rosie for leaving them alone.

She turned and started folding up the clothes. "Dad, you can't live like this. You're a mess."

"Leave those things alone," he whispered. It hurt to watch those clothes handled with such disregard, even from Jennifer, who had wept so hard at the funeral she'd nearly caved in on herself.

"I can't stay long." She continued to fold and stack Rosie's clothes, the linen shirts and the blue jeans. Her good sweaters and the silk slips she slept in. She was going to put them in boxes, drop them off at some Goodwill or resale shop. Some stranger would consider buying Rosie's favorite flannel shirt and then decide not to, without ever knowing how Rosie looked in her garden when she wore that shirt.

How it smelled when she took it off at the end of the day—like grass and dirt and spaghetti sauce. "I'm on spring break, but I've been hired to teach piano lessons at the university, so I've got a week before I have to be at school. But you can't..."

"Leave those things alone!" he yelled, and Jennifer jerked, her lips, tight and trembling. The slips fell to the floor. "Don't touch them. Don't touch anything!"

"Dad, I'm trying. I want to help."

"I don't want your help." Immediately he regretted yelling at her, but he didn't know what else to do.

Well, that wasn't true, was it? He was an alcoholic with no reason left for sobriety. No wife to love, no ability to care for the daughter who hated him.

Yes, he thought, there was always something he could do. He turned from the bedroom and stumbled down the stairs and through the kitchen to his chair. Back to the bottle and glass that were there.

Behind him—his daughter, his precious baby—followed like a bull, snorting disapproval.

"Dad, this is disgusting. You're living in filth!" She kicked aside a dirty plate.

His hands shook and half the bourbon spilled onto the chair and the floor.

"How long have you been drinking?" she asked. "Since Mom died?" He didn't answer, focused on getting the liquor into the glass. "Before that? When?"

Since the day after the doctor's appointment.

He dropped the glass and just drank from the bottle. The burn and slide of the liquor chased away the sick shakiness.

"Dad!"

He ignored her. She yelled some more. She threw something at him and it glanced off his shoulder. But he stared into nothing and drank.

It had just been a regular doctor's appointment. A physical. She hadn't been sick. Tired. Nothing. Healthy as a horse. But the blood work had shown something else, something dark and dangerous and advanced in her lungs and thyroid, and within seven months she'd been on life support.

At some point Jennifer left. And Walter sat back down in his recliner and drank with hands that shook and eyes that would not stop watering.

It had just been a damn physical.

WALTER FLOATED, reeled. And then the earth was beneath his feet with a jerk and crash. He bumped into the hospital bed and then into the monitor. His heart pounded in his ears and he couldn't get any air into his body.

"Dad," Jennifer whispered and fell into the chair beside the hospital bed. Walter swallowed and tried to find his center of gravity. His daughter was here.

Get it together, Walter.

"Dad. I'm so sorry."

Walter, clumsy and feeling too big in his own body, pushed himself between her and the bed and got down on his knees so he could see her face. "Sweetheart. Jenny." Twenty years vanished and this was his daughter before him. His baby.

She groaned and cried, muttering a constant apology.

The boy reappeared with his phone. "I found her file," he said. "She hasn't spoken to you in twenty years. That must have been a hell of a fight."

"I started drinking again." Those words sounded so

innocent, so free of the desperate and ugly reality. Walter was smiling, the muscles in his face ached from the force with which he was joyful. "But she's here. She's come back."

He stroked his daughter's face but she continued rocking with her guilt, unaware of him.

Walter had stopped drinking six months after Jennifer's visit, but it was too late. The porous remains of their relationship had evaporated. He'd reached out once, after being sober for a few months, but she'd been curt. Disbelieving. There was no way he could blame her and so he'd backed off. Gone back to the empty house and Beaverton and fiddled with his lawnmower, waiting to die.

He got letters occasionally. A picture when she eloped. But that was all.

Except now, it would seem. His daughter rocked back and forth, and finally reached out to grab his hand, the one attached to his earthly dead body.

"You did the right thing with Mom, Dad. I'm sorry I blamed you for so long. And I'm sorry I didn't try harder." Her loud, thick voice was filled with endings, with doors shutting and opportunities gone. She took a deep breath, dropped his hand, and stood. "I should have tried harder, Dad."

She walked back to the door, wiping her eyes.

"No," he breathed. "No. Where are you going?"

She opened the door and Walter turned on the boy. "Where is she going?"

"She's leaving. I don't think she intends to spend the rest of the night beside your dead body."

This couldn't be. It couldn't happen this way. He threw himself at the door in an attempt to block it, but she opened the door through him and then stepped right into where he stood, and he was nauseated with the sensation of two hearts beating in his chest. His slowing down and Jennifer's running fast.

But she walked through him, out into the hallway, and the feeling ended.

"Walter, really we need to go," the boy told him.

No. No no no no no. Twenty years and this is it? Desperately, he thought about the beat of his heart and concentrated as hard as he could, willing everything into making that heartbeat real. He focused on the physical, on the feel of the air on his skin, on the sore ache of his nose from the tubes, on the push and pull of his lungs and his heart, of the breath that came in and left. He created the sensation of sheets against his skin, a pillow under his head, the light pressure of blankets on his old body. He thought about Rosie, about his daughter. About a second chance and the things that would be different. He cataloged his regrets, highlighted his mistakes. He made promises to Rosie's Catholic God and suddenly in the silence of the hospital room the heart rate monitor beeped.

4

W alter's legs buckled and he put his hand to his knees to keep himself from falling face first on the ground. The right leg, his bad one, collapsed and he pitched sideways into something plastic and sturdy. His vision was blurred, but he knew he was no longer in the hospital. The ground beneath his feet was green. Grass? And the smell was mud and pine trees.

"Mr. Zawislak? I can not impress upon you the magnitude of the mistake you tried to make in there."

"I think I'm gonna be sick."

"Nonsense, you're dead."

"Oh God," Walter moaned, his stomach and the taste of bourbon burned in the back of his throat.

"What were you thinking, trying to jump into your body? You've been dead for an hour. Though, I must say, you managed to make your heart beat." The boy laughed a little. "I've never seen that before. Never even heard of that. The guys are not going to believe—"

Walter was on some kind of cosmic tilt-a-whirl. "Please, kid. Shut up."

"You just think you're going to be sick. Tell yourself you're fine and pay attention." He slapped Walter on the back, but the sensation of the boy's hand on his body was rather liquid. Everything was liquid except the rolling nausea in his belly.

Walter heaved himself upright and filled his body with the rain soaked air. "I'm fine," he told himself, and after a moment his vision cleared and the sickly sweet taste of imagined alcohol was gone.

Miraculously, he felt good, though his heartbeat was sluggish. He pressed his hand to his chest and could no longer feel that healthy thump and pound.

"It's your body's memory," the boy told him, and Walter finally focused on the kid. "It remembers your heart beating and your lungs taking in air and even your bad eyesight. It takes a while for the nerves to forget."

"Forget?"

"What living felt like."

That seemed reasonable. Well, as reasonable as things could seem.

"Listen, you are in a highly volatile state," the boy said. "Simply remembering an event in your life has the power to pull you back in time. You need to clear your mind of all—"

Walter was heaved sideways. Backward. He wasn't conscious of remembering anything in particular but suddenly he was in his rocker again. The fabric soft. It was new. Moonlight slid through the windows as he rocked. God, he was tired. Jennifer, a baby, an infant, was a sweet-smelling lump against his heart.

WALTER WAS DRAGGED OVER GRAVEL. Glass. Hot coals. And

then *pop!* he was in the bathroom at the Primrose Suite in that fancy hotel in Milwaukee he always stayed at for work. He was putting those travel shampoos in his kit bag to take home to Rosie.

Next time, he thought. *Next time she'll come too.*

~

WALTER WAS LIFTED from the bathroom, spun like a sock in a washing machine, and tossed down, back to earth onto his bar stool at Rudy's.

"Another?" Rudy asked, big and mean behind the bar.

"Why not?" Walter asked, having had another too many three drinks ago. It didn't matter, no one was waiting for him. He could drink himself to death. Right here.

"Walter?"

He turned sideways. A young man, a boy really, he didn't know, dressed in black and wearing thick black glasses, stood beside his stool.

"You have to come with me," he said. "You have to focus. You're dead. None of this is real."

It felt real. His buzz was certainly real, but something about that kid seemed more real.

Walter gave the beer and shot glass Rudy set down in from of him one last fond glance goodbye and closed his eyes against the pain of being jerked out of the bar.

~

AGAIN HE CRASH-LANDED against green grass that smelled of rain and pine. He rolled over to his back, wincing since every bone in his body felt abused. His muscles sore.

"I'm an old man," he protested. "I can't take this."

"You're a corpse. You'll survive." The boy laughed. "Well, not in the strict sense of the word. Or any sense, really."

"Are you, like, my guardian angel?"

"If that's comforting to you. Sure."

His angel—or whatever the hell he was—whisked his hand along the flat plastic seat of a swing and the collected water scattered, caught the light before splashing over Walter's face.

"I warned you," the boy said. He was wearing those glasses still. The big thick ones. "I told you to clear your mind."

Walter didn't even know where those memories had been kept, where they'd come from.

He sat up, his legs stretched out before him.

"Where are we?" he asked. They were no longer in the hospital. Instead it looked like they were in a small backyard.

A house and patio with sliding glass doors at one end and big fence at the other. He saw other houses over the fence, beyond the trees. Heard the sound of cars on a road, the crackle and snap of a streetcar passing.

It had just rained, and the air was cool and wet and silvery gray. The wet pine tree to his right smelled like Christmas and the grass was the greenest thing he had ever seen.

Colors look so good when you're dead.

A doll at Walter's feet had been left out and was drenched, driven into the dirt by the force of the recent rain.

"It's just a backyard," the kid said.

"How did we get here? I mean...how does all this work?"

"Trust me, the mechanics of it are quite dull."

"But what...?" He couldn't process it all. His infant daughter in his arms, the Primrose Suite. The hospital room and that feeling of being back in his body. Of wanting so badly to talk to Jennifer. It had been stupid, but it had been real in a way the last twenty years of his life had not. "Was that it? Were those the days I relived?"

"No. As I tried to explain earlier, your body is liquid, mist, a puddle." The boy looked heavenward. "All the earthly constraints of physics and natural law don't apply to you now. You can go wherever—or maybe I should say, *whenever* in your life. The curtain has lifted and if we're ever going to get through this, you must give me control. I have a list. I have a protocol. It's much simpler if you just—"

"Fine," Walter said, happy as always to give up control. "You're in charge."

The boy nodded and punched something into his phone. *Powerful things those phones.* "Now, I must warn you about the pain. It will come and go, and when it comes, it will get worse."

He was used to pain. His hip throbbed even now.

"The more days you go back to visit. The more days you remember without fully accepting your life and your death, the more it's going to hurt."

"I thought this was supposed to be a gift to dead people. Sounds like torture."

"Just trying to help you decide."

The boy grabbed the phone from his pocket, consulting the screen with a furrowed brow.

"Now, you get to remember the days on my list before making a choice." He looked at Walter through his lashes. "We found that most people over forty-five couldn't remember half of what had happened to them, and if they could actually recall the event they wanted to relive they got the date all wrong. In any case, the list and visits make things much more tidy. You'll be in your body, as you were, not as you are now."

The opportunity that presented itself was dizzying. He turned to the boy who flickered and winked in the strange, liquid air.

"I know what day I want to relive."

"You sure? We haven't really gone through the list yet."

"I don't need the list. I want the day Jennifer came home from school. I want to go back and..."

"Fix something?"

"Exactly." If he was sober when Jennifer showed up, and if he just talked to her and listened to her, the whole rest of his life, even his death, might be different. Memories realigned, changing even as he thought about them, and the things he tried to forget were smaller, mutable, but fixing things with his daughter was a solid and real possibility.

The boy shook his head. "No can do."

"What?"

"There's no going back for you, Walter. For anyone. You get to relive a day but you can't change it."

Suddenly, from the rich soil at their feet, a green aluminum filing cabinet erupted, sending clumps of grass and dirt into the air. A door slid out and the kid removed a manila folder. He hummed and flipped through the pages. Finally he grimaced and pointed at something on one of the faded cream pages.

"See, you'd change that day, but the next day you'll wake up on the bathroom floor, drunk and sick just like you did the first time around. It took you six months to stop drinking, and changing one day won't fix that." He flipped another page. "Jennifer will start the systematic removal of you from her life, no matter what happens on the day you go back to relive. You can't change anything." The boy shrugged.

Walter's hopes, which had gone up into the stratosphere, crashed and he stepped back and ran into the bright yellow plastic slide again.

"Oh!" the boy continued. "And you can't tell people to buy Google stock or bet on the Cubs for the World Series. Lots of people tried that." He returned the folder to the drawer and the whole thing descended back into the soil, the earth repairing itself like it had never given birth to an aluminum filing cabinet.

The world swam. Walter stumbled again, and the slide was at his back. The boy put his hand on Walter's arm, something Walter could barely feel, like the light brush of a breeze rather than flesh and bone. "I'm sorry, Walter. It doesn't work. Life goes on just like it did. No changes. No do-overs."

"So what's the point?" Walter asked, bitterness pouring from his mouth. "Why do this if we can't change anything?"

The boy looked surprised. "Well, I suppose it's not about changing your life. It's about appreciating it. That's why we do this. To remind you of what you've forgotten."

Walter looked up at the Technicolor sky with the carousing clouds and felt a yawning desolation in his chest.

"I haven't forgotten anything," he said. "Just let me go. I don't want to stick around. I don't want to watch what happens on Earth. I just want..." Walter hauled in a deep breath and felt suddenly every moment of his age. "I'm just tired."

The boy sucked his teeth. "No can do. Policy. Just let me show you what you've forgotten. It's beautiful. Every moment, even the bad ones, have something redeemable."

"You have the wrong file."

"You can go back and see your wife."

Walter spun, got dizzy, and braced himself against the slide.

"I don't want to see her."

The boy watched him carefully with dark, dour eyes and then smiled, and the smile made Walter think that the kid knew more than he did. The boy reminded him of his cousin Dan. Who'd been too worldly for the rest of the Zawislak family.

"All right. There has to be something you don't mind re-experiencing. How about one more day of sleeping or eating…" The boy's voice was that low, melodious soothe Walter remembered from the gray hallway, and Walter felt the slow bob up of his emotions. His anger thinned out.

Walter's stomach growled, his not quite dead nerves making their presence known. Rosie had always said he'd miss his own funeral for a buffet.

"There you go. I've heard bacon truly lives up to its reputation. It's all you heart-attack victims can talk about."

"Does it have to be *my* life?" Walter asked. "I mean, can I choose someone more interesting? Can I be Neil Armstrong?"

"Sorry, you can go back to the day you watched Neil Armstrong on the moon, but you can't be that guy. It's all very tricky."

Again Walter deflated.

"Most people are quite excited about this. One lady wanted to go back and watch Princess Di's wedding again, can you believe it?" The boy prattled on while Walter tried to think of a day he wanted to most relive, but they were all a blur, smudged by time and distance. "One guy wanted to relive the day he stole his dad's Porsche and ran it into a tree.

You can do anything." The boy raised a long slender finger. "Except change things."

The boy sat down on the swing and began to pump his legs, and the swing gained height. The boy soared over Walter's head, far higher than earthly swing set chains could go. He swung up and eclipsed the sun, which was struggling behind clouds.

The wild emotions left Walter tired and he sat down on the plastic step of the slide.

He wished that at some point in his life he had stolen a Porsche.

Maybe there wasn't much to change. There was nothing to rage against and he found himself doing what he had learned best after he stopped drinking. Accepting. Things are what they are.

He'd been in AA for most of his life. He'd repeated that Serenity Prayer every day without fully knowing what it meant. He had to lose his wife, his daughter, start drinking again, and then stop because of shame before those words made any freaking sense to him.

Accept what I cannot change.

Jennifer had come back. It wasn't enough by any means; it didn't erase the years of silent standoff, it didn't give him back whatever he had missed of her in those years. But it was *something*. And that was so much more than what he'd had dying alone in that bed.

His daughter was sorry and she forgave him, and the stones of remorse and regret were lifted from around his neck.

He rubbed his hands over his face, scrubbed at his eyes.

One thing was sure; death so far was nothing like what he had been told. Movies, Father Kennedy, the bible stories —none of them even suggested that gray hallway or the kid.

The boy was still swinging, reaching impossible heights. He was higher than the house whose yard they were trespassing in and the neighboring houses. He was taller than the pine trees and suddenly the boy leaped from his swing and Walter gasped, lurching to his feet.

The boy floated, took two steps off the roof, and somersaulted in the air. He lost his shape; his outline wavered and faded in milky sunshine and suddenly reappeared right in front of Walter.

The kid no longer wore black; instead, he was in a pair of chinos, a madras shirt, and Chuck Taylors. He was a *Life* magazine photo of the 60s brought to life.

Walter felt an odd quiver, and when he looked down he realized he had traded in his robe and slippers for a short-sleeved dress shirt and brown striped tie just like the ones he had been wearing to work for the past thirteen years. He used to be a very reluctant suit-and-tie man, but after he drank away the promotion he'd grown to like a little pomp and circumstance. It was a warehouse and he could have worn a sweatshirt like the employees, but he thought the tie said something. What, he wasn't sure.

"You look good, kid,"

The boy smiled and looked down at his vintage ensemble.

"Thanks. I always thought this look had a lot going for it."

"Who are you?" Walter asked.

"My name is Peter."

Walter gasped. He'd been swearing at a saint? Rosie would kill him. "I'm sorry...Saint Peter, I had no—"

The boy snorted. "You Catholics kill me, you really do. Yeah, I'm Saint Peter Goldstein." He ducked his head and

Walter saw a black skullcap nestled in the dark curls of his head.

"You're Jewish?" Walter hadn't paid a whole lot of attention in church, but he was fairly sure that Father Kennedy at St. Mary of the Angel's Catholic Church in Beaverton, Wisconsin, would be flabbergasted to see Peter Goldstein manning the Pearly Gates.

"Well, my mother was. Dad converted." Peter began walking away from Walter toward the sliding glass door of the house and Walter took a few running steps to catch up. "Ravi was supposed to have your file, but since you're two days early and Ravi was dealing with the earthquake in China, I got you."

"Ravi?" Walter couldn't quite follow this. "This is heaven, right?"

"Sort of. It's what you folks call Limbo."

"And Ravi…"

"Hindu. Nice guy. Heaven is whatever you want, but Limbo…" The boy winked. "We get everyone."

"So everyone goes to heaven? We all get redemption in the afterlife." Walter remembered the years spent in confession on his knees, worried that the thoughts he had about MaryAnn Arneson were going to land him in the fiery pits. The years after the war when he was sure the blood on his hands had soaked right through to his soul.

Man, won't Father Kennedy just blow a fuse when he gets here.

"Church? Confession? All that stuff. I was right? None of it matters?"

The kid shot him a skeptical look. "When, Walter Zawislak, was the last time you were in church?"

Walter stood up straight. He swallowed hard, tugging at words rooted in the back of his throat. "There's no benevolent father watching over us. I know this. I am proof that God is vindictive. So save your preaching."

"There is nothing more tiresome than a philosophical discussion with a man who has forgotten his faith." Peter deepened his voice an octave in a way Walter could only assume was making fun of him. "*Show me. Prove it.* You doubters never get it."

"Get what?"

"There's no proof." Peter shrugged. "It's faith. It's the step off the cliff into the ether. And it doesn't matter what you put your faith in, a holy spirit or the beauty of mankind, faith is faith."

"Well, Rosie was the one with faith."

The boy stared at him long and hard, and again Walter felt uncomfortable with this gaze, like the kid was seeing past his flesh and bone into those places hidden and dark and lost to him a million years ago.

"You have a decision to make, Walter. And I..." he looked back down at the beeper at his side "...have a two o'clock with the lamentable result of a bad piece of fish."

Right. The business of reliving one day.

The vertical blinds on the other side of the glass door shimmied and a little girl appeared, her dark face pressed flat against the glass.

Walter jerked and looked to hide before he remembered he was not visible to that girl. She lifted her arm and pulled with all of her weight. The seal on the door popped and it slid open.

"It stopped raining, Mom!" the girl yelled. She looked like she was about eight years old, her hair pulled back into two ponytails on the top of her head.

"Wear your boots!" a woman shouted back and Walter

smiled, reminded of Rosie and Jennifer during his daughter's young, pleasant years.

"Who are these people?" Walter asked. The little girl pulled on a pair of pink rain boots and slicker that matched and charged out into the damp air.

"I've never met them," Peter said.

Walter turned to look at Peter, but from the corner of his eye he saw where there had only been one tree, suddenly there were two and then four. All the trees began to multiply and grow. The single spruce became a forest of long established trees that knit themselves together to create a thick canopy. The swing set vanished and a large granite overhang replaced it, part of the Northern Shield. Roots grew under Walter's feet, slithering like snakes underneath the brown pine needles and rotting leaves that hadn't been there before.

The sky opened up past the tops of the trees, like a soaring cathedral ceiling. Clouds seemed taller and the air suddenly tasted good. Like pine and wood smoke. The house faded to mist and a river ran beneath it, babbling over rocks, glittering in the sun that moved from its western slope to just above the eastern horizon.

"What's going on?" Walter asked, panicked.

5

"It's morning," Peter said.

"Morning where?" Walter stumbled as rocks slowly bubbled and solidified beneath his feet.

Peter turned, searched the north for something, and out of air, wind, and whatever magic this boy controlled, Walter's grandparents' cabin appeared on the bluff overlooking the river.

Nostalgic, little-boy wonder, something he'd long ago forgotten he'd ever experienced, manifested itself from the dying remains of his earthly emotions. "We're in Minnesota," Walter said.

And just like that, the drone of a thousand mosquitoes filled the air. Black flies the size of sparrows orbited his head but never landed.

"Lovely," Peter muttered, swatting at the sudden swarm.

"But what are we doing here?"

Peter handed him the sheet. "It's the first day on your list."

He and his folks and brother had vacationed dozens of times up here over the years, but the date printed in black and white meant nothing to him. Could have been any one of those vacations.

"I don't—"

"Here they come."

Leaves rustled behind him and Walter turned to find, emerging from the pine trees to stand on the granite over-hang, his father, Vicktor, his brother, Christopher, and cousin Dan, and finally bringing up the rear—himself.

"Holy shit!" Walter cried. "That's me."

"That's the idea."

They all had fishing poles and tackle boxes. Christopher wore the hat Dad had given him with the lures tucked in the band. It was too big. He had to keep pushing the hat out of his face, his fingers constantly pricked by the lures.

Walter had no such hat.

"God, look at me." Walter approached his young self. He was a child. A baby. Though, from the view of his ankle over his Chuck Taylors and below the hem of his blue jeans, he'd experienced a heck of a growth spurt recently.

Always tall, always skinny, he looked startlingly so in whatever odd hindsight this was. His hands holding his fishing pole looked awkward or vulnerable, too big on the whip-thin bamboo pole. Not a boy's hands and far from being a man's hands, but the first taste of the ungainly teenage years to come.

Walter still couldn't place this day. Fishing at the cabin with his dad and brother was a pretty common occurrence. The fact that Dan was there and that his right arm ended in a stump just below the elbow made it a summer after July 4, 1954.

"What's so special about this day? I mean I like fishing, but..."

"You used to dream about this day." Peter walked

through branches as if they weren't there. "When you got older. You dreamed about this day more than anything else."

"Really?" Walter ducked under a broken tree limb and realized he had no head to hit. Old habits, dying hard. "I don't remember that dream."

"Most people don't."

"But if it's important, you'd think I'd remember."

"You'd think."

Fishing, he thought, with real uncompromised pleasure. *Why the hell not?*

Peter hit a button on his mysterious remote with his thumb, and like a rope had been tied around Walter's waist and then yanked with the force of a dozen horses, Walter was jerked backward. He folded in on himself, squeezed and squashed until it hurt. Until he thought his eardrums would burst and his nose would bleed. And then the pressure was gone and he lost the sensation of his body.

Walter floated. Like something cut loose in the wind—leaves or a plastic bag from the grocery store. He twirled and dropped and then was tossed high again, and then it seemed the wind ceased blowing and he...just...stopped.

6

J une 12, 1956
    Wabash, Minnesota
    Eastern Bank of the Kettle River

"LET'S SPLIT UP," Vicktor said, eyeing the river beneath them like a battleground. "Dan and Walter, you guys head north. Christopher and I will go south."

"I don't want to go south—" Christopher whined, and Walter held his breath. *Holy Crap, Christopher, it's like you want to get smacked.*

"I didn't ask you what you want, did I?" Vicktor didn't even look at Christopher.

"No sir," Christopher whispered, and under his mustache Dad's lips twitched in a smile. Slowly, Walter let out that breath.

It had been a good morning so far, but Christopher's whining could ruin everything.

"Remember," Dad said, looking over at Walter with his cold, hard eyes.

Don't flinch, he thought. *Don't look away.*

"You don't catch anything, you don't eat anything."

He said it like he already expected Walter to come up empty. *I'm good*, he wanted to shout. *I'm patient and careful and I'm better than Christopher, not that you notice.*

But what he said was, "Yes sir," and nodded at Dan before stepping through the trees along a deer path that ran beside the river.

They walked for about twenty minutes until the trail ended at a granite lip that jutted out into a small set of rapids. Dan dug something out of his pocket and sat down, leaning against a dead tree stump, his pole forgotten at his side.

Walter stepped up to the water and made a big show of looking through his tackle box, but mostly he watched Dan out of the corner of his eye. Dan could still roll a cigarette even though he didn't have his right hand. Mom said he had to be nice and not stare, but Jesus. Dan was rolling a cigarette with one hand!

"You want one?" Dan asked, holding out the finished product of his efforts.

"No," Walter muttered and peered back into his tackle box, moving things around like he hadn't been watching, his heart beating hard against his ribs.

Dan made him nervous these days and it wasn't just the hand. He'd turned fifteen this year. And seemed different because of it. Like he knew things Walter would never know.

Dan pulled a lighter from the pocket of his blue jeans and lit the cigarette.

They used to be friends. They'd ride bikes to each

other's houses after school. But now...Walt didn't know what they were.

Just cousins, maybe.

"Your dad must hate you," Dan said. He pulled a flake of tobacco off his tongue and squinted at Walter.

"No, he doesn't." Walter selected a mayfly lure and tucked his pole between his knees so he could tie the little bit of feathers and plastic to his line.

"He always puts you with me."

"So?"

"Well..." Dan chortled. "He definitely hates me, so I figure that's why he puts us together."

"He doesn't hate you," Walter said, but he couldn't be sure. Dad really acted like he didn't like Dan. Always had. Which didn't make any sense considering Dan used to be the nicest guy. He still was nice, he just wasn't...polite, maybe. The guy was smart. He could jump higher than anyone else at the high school, he'd even made the varsity basketball team as a freshman. But Dad always treated Dan like he'd done something wrong.

"Christopher's little, is all." He took the line between his forefinger and thumb and cast into the still area around the rocks just this side of the rapids. The fish liked those places best.

"Christopher can't fish!" Dan cried and started laughing. "Your Dad gave him that hat and Christopher hates it!"

"That's not true." Walter looked over his shoulder at Dan. But it was. Christopher didn't like the bugs and he said that Dad was too mean to make it fun. Dad made it hard.

Which was true, but that's the way Dad did everything.

"Why didn't he give you the hat?" Dan asked. "You love fishing."

Walter swallowed and pulled his line a bit, jerking the

lure to attract something, anything that might end this dumb conversation.

He liked the hat. The lures Dad had taken all that time to tie and put on the band glittered and gleamed in the sunshine. It was a serious hat. A great hat.

"It was Christopher's birthday," Walter muttered. Mom told him he needed to be kind to his brother. But he wanted to take that hat. Christopher didn't treat it well, he left it balled up under his bed, but Walter always pulled it out and hung it over the lamp so the lures wouldn't get tangled and the hat kept its shape.

"So?" Dan tapped the ash from the cigarette beside him on the stone.

"So what?"

"Why doesn't he like you?"

"He likes me just fine! Why doesn't he like you?"

Dan blinked. And then smiled and shrugged like the answer didn't really matter to him. "I don't know."

Walter swallowed the ball of guilt. He shouldn't have said anything. They didn't talk about the accident. After the fight between Dad and Uncle Mark, not even Grandma talked about "poor Dan."

"The thing with the firecracker was an accident, you know," he felt compelled to say.

"You sure about that?" Dan looked down at his cigarette as he ground it into the stone. He pulled his supplies out and started assembling another one.

"He thought it was a dud."

"Good," Dan smiled. "Everyone should believe good things about their dads." He nodded out toward Walt's line. "I think you just got robbed."

Walt turned and started reeling in. Sure enough, his hook was empty and his lure was gone. Damn it!

"I'm going to take a nap," Dan said.

Walter didn't say anything, he tied on a new lure, slung back his arm, let his elbow and wrist go fluid like Dad taught him, and set the lure spiraling out through the sunlight and swarms of mosquitoes that hovered over the still places on the river. He got it as close as he could to the rapids and then, like he'd been taught, he waited.

He counted trees on the opposite bank of the river.

He stood in one spot as long as he could, counting to a hundred, sometimes a hundred and ten, and then he shifted and started all over again.

He named all the states that began with the letter A and all the countries that started with the letter C.

And then, just as the heat and the drone of the bugs began to wear on him, lull him into boredom and weariness, his line went taut and the tip of his rod bent so far it almost touched the water.

He was pulled off balance, but he quickly braced his legs and leaned back, reeling as fast as the mechanism allowed, bracing the butt of the rod in his belly, right at the top of his jeans.

Oh man, it was a big one.

The muscles in his back burned and the rod in his belly felt like it might push all the way through his gut. He bit his lip and reeled as hard as he could until finally he saw the trout on the end of his line. A sleek shadow that darted left and zagged right.

A monster. A big, giant monster.

Walter took three steps backward, and putting his entire body into it, he pulled that fish in, reeling and tugging as hard as he could until it landed, panting and flopping on the stone.

A footer for sure.

The hook had caught the fish right through the gills and Walter knew there could be no careful freeing of this fish. He stepped on its slithery body and yanked the hook out.

Blood sprayed across the stone and the fish's flopping slowed. Walter watched until it stopped moving and reminded himself of what his science teacher told him—fish don't feel it.

He grabbed the wicker creel his mom had made him last Christmas. She made one for him, Dad, and Chris, each of them different so they wouldn't get confused. Walt's was yellow cane with a big brown W on the lid.

Happy with every aspect of that fish—its beautiful coloring, its superior size and weight, the tremendous fight it gave him—he tucked it into his basket.

It was a very fine fish.

Walt tied on another June bug and recast, and then the real fun began.

It was the best day of fishing he'd ever had. He couldn't miss. He never lost another lure and never had to wait more than a minute for a nibble. It was like the fish were just lining up waiting for him.

It was an epic day, not even his dad could have done so well.

Two hours later, muscles sore but with ten beautiful keepers tucked into the wicker creel slung over his shoulder, Walter kicked his cousin awake.

"Let's go find Dad," he said.

"You catch something?" Dan asked, pushing himself upright.

"Boy, did I," Walter said with a grin. "I've got dinner and breakfast for the rest of the weekend." He swung the box around to his waist and lifted the lid to show Dan his catch.

They were gorgeous. Green and black and rainbow

colored along their lean bellies where the sunlight hit them. Each one of them as long as his forearm.

Dan smiled like the cousin Walter remembered. "Good, I'm starved!"

Walter led them back toward the spot where they'd split up and then he kept going south along the deer trail. He imagined his father would take Christopher toward the falls, so he ignored the mosquitoes, drunk and hungry on the smell of the blood that seeped from the basket down his pants leg, and pressed on.

He could hear Dan behind him, cursing.

"You can stop," he said. "Head on back to the cabin."

"And miss seeing your dad when you show him those fish! Forget it," Dan said, his face red and wet with sweat.

Walter grinned, swallowing the delighted little chirp he felt in the back of his throat.

They broke out of the forest onto the edge of the river, just above the falls. The falls weren't anything big, just a foot-tall drop. Christopher sat on the granite, his legs curled into his chest, scratching at his ankles like he wanted to touch bone.

"Chris! What's wrong?" Walter asked. He looked for the long shadow cast by his father but he wasn't around. "Where's Dad?"

"He got mad and left," Christopher muttered. He'd been crying, and crying hard from the looks of him.

And his lip was split. Dad's ring could do that if he hit you just right.

"You okay?" Dan pulled out his canteen and handed it to Christopher, who opened the screw cap and took huge gulps of the water like he'd been dying in the desert.

The idiot was sitting next to a river; if he was thirsty he could have just dunked his face into the water.

Walter shook his head like Dad did when Christopher or Walter did something dumb.

"You're such a whiney baby," Walter said. "That's why he hits you. You gotta learn to keep your mouth shut."

He didn't want to carry the fish any farther. They were heavy and the strap of the creel dug into his shoulder and hurt. Not to mention the black flies that followed him like a cloud.

"Which way did he go?"

Chris pointed south.

"To the big bend?" Walter asked, and Christopher nodded.

It was too far to walk. Walter shrugged out of the strap and set the fish in the cool shallow water closest to the bank. At least they'd stay fresh.

"We'll wait here, then," he said, splashing water onto his face. He felt like a grown-up saying such things. Saying such things with ten fish in his creel. He smiled at his distorted reflection in the water. "Did you catch anything?" Walter asked.

Christopher kicked over his empty wicker creel.

"Every time we go fishing he gets mad at me," Christopher began to wail. "It's not my fault I'm no good at it."

"Of course not," Dan said, and Walter wanted to tell Dan not to encourage Christopher. That it wouldn't help him in the long run. Christopher just had to become a better fisherman, that's all there was to it. He had to learn to ignore the bugs and the heat, or Dad would just get meaner.

"Give me your creel," Walter said.

Christopher reached out his foot and kicked it closer to Walter. Walter scowled at him. "You're acting like a baby. No wonder Dad left."

Christopher scowled back and Walter headed over to his creel in the shallows.

He was going to just put a few of his fish into Christopher's so it would look like he'd caught something, and then maybe Dad would leave him alone. But—that would diminish the day Walt'd had. Ten fish—each of them more beautiful than the last. Someone deserved to have the bragging rights to a day like this.

If Walt didn't have any fish, Dad would turn on him, call him a waste. Or maybe he wouldn't. Maybe, excited for Christopher, proud of the little kid whom everyone (except Dad) knew hated going to the river, he wouldn't even notice what Walter did or didn't catch.

Christopher was just a kid. Walter, as of today, was a guy who took care of his family. Caught them dinner when they were hungry.

"What are you doing, Walt?" Chris asked.

"Giving you my fish."

"All the fish?" Dan asked and then hooted. "Your Dad won't believe Chris caught all them himself."

"Sure he will," Walt said. He carefully lifted each slithery body out of his basket and into his brother's. Drops of blood fell onto the stone and ran into the water, attracting little minnows along with water striders and other bugs. He swatted at a horsefly.

Maybe he would believe it. Or maybe not. Walter guessed he would. Dad believed the best in Christopher— saw things that just weren't there—he'd given him that hat, after all.

"Walt?" Chris asked, beside him. He had mosquito bites on his legs that had swollen up like acorns. Poor guy, he really did hate this.

"Yeah, Chris."

"Thanks."

"You're welcome."

"Hey!" Dan cried, and both Walt and Chris turned to look at him. He stripped down to his drawers and tennis shoes. "Last one in is a rotten egg!" He streaked past them and charged into the river, sending spray into the air and scaring away every fish for miles.

Walter laughed, tore off his shirt and pants, and hurled himself into the river after Dan, the cool water hit his body and fixed him. It made the itch go away, the heat and the regret that his dad probably would never guess the day he'd had fishing.

"Come on, Chris," he said, turning back to his brother, so small and thin on the edge of the river. "The water's great!"

He cupped his hand and smacked the surface sending a wave over the rock and into the sunshine, where for a brief second it turned to diamonds and then fell, just water again, back to the river.

7

Walter was sucked back out of that summer day with the force of a hurricane using a straw, and he landed, sick and spinning against the metal bars of the swing set.

He stumbled, righted himself, and stumbled again, the world a mad tilt-a-whirl.

Finally, he just lay down. The green grass poked him through his shirt.

"Holy hell," he muttered up the blue sky that continued to spin. "I think I'm motion sick."

"Nonsense, you're not moving anywhere."

Walter sought out Peter, found him peering down at him from the top of the slide.

"So?" Peter asked. "A day of fishing. Selfless heroics for your brother—care to relive it all? The taste of fried fish you'd caught yourself?" Peter waggled his eyebrows and held out a sheaf of papers.

"What's that?"

"A contract."

"There are contracts in heaven?"

"Nope." Peter shook his head. "But we got plenty in limbo. So? What do you say? Care to relive that day?"

Walter shook his head and turned back to the sky. Blue and holding still. Thank God. "Not really."

"Did your dad believe that Chris caught those fish?"

Walter closed his eyes, burped river water, and nodded.

"Sorry."

Walter shrugged. It had been the beginning of something, that day, or the end of something, really. Nothing was ever the same after that with his dad. And Walter had spent a lot of years trying to change it back, but it was too late. And he was the only one trying. Dad didn't seem to notice.

"What's the next day on that list?" Walt asked.

Walter turned to Peter but the boy was no longer on the slide. Instead there was a big heavy purple door with a metal push bar standing in the middle of the lawn.

The muffled roar of a crowd, the flat electronic buzzer of a clock, and the unmistakable slap and squeak of rubber soles on a gym floor leaked out from under the door.

Walter slowly got to his feet.

"What is that?"

Peter ducked out from behind the door, something glad and devilish in his gaze. "I think it's basketball."

Basketball had been the game of Walter's teenage years. He'd loved it, even though he was too short and too slow to really be good. But as Mr. Kerestes, his old basketball coach, used to say, he played like a bulldog when other guys played like poodles.

"Check the second date on the list." Peter pointed to the list of dates that magically appeared in Walter's hand.

"I'm sixty-six years old, Peter. I can't remember these dates."

"Well..." The boy put his hand on the push bar of the

heavy dark door. "The second day on that list is on the other side of this door."

Walter smiled and actually felt a bubble of laughter in his gullet. This might be kind of fun.

"Well, lead on, Peter Goldstein."

And they walked through the door.

The smell of the old gymnasium was overpowering and nostalgic. Those old wooden and concrete gyms held sweat and heat like hotboxes. And the noise! Buzzers and screams and the cheerleaders in their heavy wool skirts and sweaters, and the crowd...

Walter turned to look up into the stands at the hundreds of Beaverton citizens who had come out to see their beloved Screaming Eagles win the state championship.

This day had been forgotten in the living of long years, in the press of far more serious things than a high school basketball games, but it wobbled to the surface of Walter's memory attached to a feeling that had also been lost in the years. Excitement. Gut-clenching, heart-pounding excitement.

"Holy shit," he breathed.

Walter blinked, wondering when the hell his vision would sort itself out. The color of the air...of the court... Walter couldn't be sure but all the colors were faded and watery, like an early Kodachrome photograph. Like the photo of this team that had been taken after the game for the paper.

A boy rushed by, dribbling down court like a thing of beauty and grace. He took the two steps to the basket, made that light, airy leap, that twist and stretch, and the ball tipped off his fingers onto the backboard and into the basket.

Al Torreno. Man, Walter hadn't thought about that kid

in years. He'd gone on to play college ball but Walter didn't know what happened to him after that. Probably killed in some rice paddy in Southeast Asia like most of the kids on that court.

Man oh man, look at these guys. Walter laughed. Gangly green boys who thought that whatever happened on that court, that night, would make or break them.

For Walter, that had been particularly true.

"This has to be the whitest basketball team ever," Peter said.

Walter nodded.

Peter ran out from behind Walter, to the edge of the court. He waited, hopping on his toes. "This is my favorite!" Peter cried.

Lou Crimell approached with his distinctive lurching gait. Peter took one long, leaping step sideways as Lou whipped past and Peter seemed to get swept up in the current created by Lou's body. Peter became a glittering phantom aura surrounding Lou.

Lou pivoted and took off the other way, and Peter was left weaving and smiling like a drunk at center court.

"You okay, kid?"

"So good." Peter jogged over to where Walter stood in the shadows of the stands. "You guys always take the best things for granted."

"Who?"

"You recently deceased."

"What things do we take for granted?"

"Sweating. Being out of breath. Knee pain. Blisters. And running." He sighed in ecstasy. "Running is the best."

"You run." Walter looked down at Peter's feet, which he realized weren't actually on the ground. Peter was sort of floating, his Chuck Taylors a few inches off the polished pine floor.

"Well, I'll be damned," Walter murmured. "Why do you wear shoes?"

Peter blinked at him. "I don't know. I like them, I guess."

"Anybody ever tell you you're an odd duck?"

"Anybody ever tell you you're a grumpy old man?"

"No, actually."

"Well, let me be the first."

Lou bobbled a rebound and turned over the ball. The Whitewater player took it to the basket and, luckily, missed.

Peter gazed out at the court, his lips pursed. "So which one are you?"

Water laughed, a hard bark, and remembered what this was about. He was out there somewhere and he really wasn't sure if he was ready to see the seventeen-year-old version of himself.

But curiosity got the best of him and he searched for himself on the court, among all the teenagers with the same shorts and long socks and buzz-cut hair. The Whitewater players in their blue uniforms made a fast break toward their own basket and there he was, bringing up the rear.

The shortest, slowest point guard maybe in the history of the game. His nose had already been bloodied; he could see sweaty dark splotches where he had wiped it on his number 10 jersey. He had been giving that Whitewater player a rough time and in the third quarter Walter got an elbow in the nose for his troubles. But oh, the fourth quarter. He looked up at the clock and saw that the third was winding down.

Like a ten-year-old he hopped around the corner of the stands and turned to get a front row seat for one of the greatest moments in his life. As he sat he had that strange sensation of falling into something or down something only to land in the memory of the fourth quarter of the 1962 Wisconsin State Finals.

MARCH 11, 1962

Ten seconds left in the fourth quarter of the Wisconsin State Basketball Finals

Beaverton High School Gymnasium

WALT LANDED hard on his butt and tasted blood where he'd bitten his tongue.

"That's a foul, ref!" he yelled, but the ref didn't listen. Instead, he pointed a finger at Walt and shouted, "You are walking a thin line, Zawislak."

Walt slowly made his way to his feet. Owens, the Whitewater player who'd just about broke Walt's tailbone, grinned and winked at him.

"Screw you!" Walt shouted at the kid.

"Zawislak!" It was Kerestes at the bench. "Cool it."

The rolls of fat over Kerestes' bow tie turned purple; the guy sweated blood. And everybody in that gymnasium was going bonkers.

There were ten seconds left in the game and Beaverton was down by two. And Walt was all too aware that he was a senior. This was his last chance.

He looked up at the third row of the Beaverton Stands on the right side and quickly found his parents. His mother looked worried, like a distressed hen in a blue dress. His father of course, looked bigger than any person around him and like his top was going to blow right off.

Vicktor Zawislak jerked his thumb at the Whitewater basket. "Get off your ass and go after 'em," he yelled.

Walt wiped his runny, bleeding nose on his jersey and trotted toward the action under the Whitewater basket. Sometimes he wished his father wouldn't even come to these things.

Al Torreno caught the rebound and fired the ball at Micky Stuts, who got midcourt before the giants of Whitewater were all over him. The defense had been on them like flies on shit all damn game. There was nothing the Beaverton guys could do to get to the basket without fouling one of the Whitewater players. Walt had four personal fouls already and if things didn't ease up here real quick Walt was going to foul that Owens asshole all the way to the hospital.

Stuts pivoted twice, searching between the arms and grabbing hands of his Whitewater guard for someone, anyone who was open.

He felt his father's dark eyes boring into his back, searing his skin and branding his bones.

Go. Go now or the old man will never let me forget it.

Walt faked right but deked left and managed to get Owens behind him. He threw a hard shot to Owens's ribs with his elbow just to remind him who he was dealing with.

Three seconds left.

Walt lurched to his favorite spot, his sweet spot at a forty-five degree angle from the basket on the left-hand side.

"Over here, Mick," he shouted.

Micky fired an overhead pass and Walt caught it at his chest, the ball slippery in his sweaty hands. He turned, his right foot planted all the way into the center of the earth and the ball rolled to the tips of his fingers.

Two seconds left.

The basket from this position, this sweet spot, was the

Grand Canyon. Owens was there, but so was the tick of the clock counting the final seconds of his basketball career, ticking away his chances to be a champion.

One second left.

Walt jumped, his muscles firing and he was lifted up high at the apex of his jump shot. Higher than Owens. Higher than Al. Higher than he'd ever been, and the ball made its beautiful graceful arc, its spin fast and steady.

But he knew, he knew before the ball left his hands, it wasn't going in. It was too far right.

He'd blown it.

Before his feet touched the ground Owens was there and he clipped Walt right under the chin with his elbow. Walt went down hard just as the buzzer rang and the ball bounced off the rim.

"Foul!" Al Torreno screamed.

The world swam and the racket of the crowd and the buzzer and the whistles all swelled and swirled then dimmed in his ears. He had to rest his head against the fixed surface of the court.

Man, he really got me.

He could see Kerestes going nuts at the bench but there was no sound, and Walt knew that was weird but he really didn't care. If he turned his head nice and easy so the world didn't go spinning into orbit, he saw his mom and dad. It looked like Mom was ready to come running out of the stands to take on Owens herself, but Dad had her elbow.

He smiled, trying to let her know he was fine, or would be soon, that she shouldn't worry. His father's face turned red and Walt could read his lips as he shouted, "Get up!"

Right. Get up. He closed his eyes and they rolled up under his eyelids. The floor began to spin and he wondered if he was going to barf just as he was suddenly yanked to his feet.

"Let's go! Walt!" It was Al, his face red and shining with sweat and purpose. "We can win this, you've got two plus a T."

"Technical foul?" He coughed the words.

"Damn right foul!" Al's breath was hot and wet on Walt's face, and he wondered again if he was going to puke. "Look man!" Al pointed to the score.

Beaverton trailed by two, no time on the clock, and Walt had three free throws.

Walt burped bile.

The world careened back into place and he had that pop in his ears, like when they drove up the big hill when they went to go visit his mom's folks in Red Lodge, Minnesota, and he could hear again, the clamoring crowd. He shook off the dizziness, the otherworldliness that the cheap shot had given him, and he focused on the feel of his heart in his chest and the sweat stinging his eyes.

Get it together. Walt. Get it together.

"You ready, Zawislak?"

Walt nodded and caught the bounce pass from the ref who stood at the baseline under the basket.

His teammates, Lou, Al, Bear, and Micky, all stood at the half line and Walt was all alone at the foul line. The Whitewater team looked like they were gonna piss themselves or cry, and Walt couldn't help but turn and wink at Owens where he stood, smoke coming out of his ears.

If Walt got all three of these Owens would never live it down. Ever. It was better than giving him a black eye.

Walt felt the moment out, pressed on the edges of what he had dreamed of a million times in his bed at night. The dream didn't come with the churning guts and the creepy sensation of hundreds of eyes watching him dribble the ball, trying to relax.

The truth was, he was fucking scared, and he'd feel a whole lot better if Al shot these free throws.

But at least it was free throws. He could do these with his eyes closed. His father used to field countless rebounds for him off the basket over the garage door.

Do it again, his father said when it was getting dark.

Do it again, his father said when his mother called them in for dinner.

Again, you baby, his father said when Walt complained that he was tired and he couldn't see, or he was bored and wanted to watch *I Love Lucy*.

Walt drank deep of the warm sweaty air, eyed the basket, and put the ball in the air.

It went in with a clean, sweet swish.

Beaverton behind by one.

The boys all leaned in and clapped his hand and smacked his butt.

Walt dared a glance up at the stands. One quick look at the old man who stood with his arms crossed, chewing on the ends of his mustache.

His mom covered her face with her hands.

The ref blew the whistle and passed the ball to him.

"You can do it, Walt!" a girl yelled, and the crowd roared, and suddenly, like lightning, Walt was nervous.

Not just a little, but a shaky legs, loose guts, sweaty palms kind of nervous.

He tried to push the noise of the crowd away and forced himself to imagine the gym was his driveway. It was dusk and the smell of sausages floated out of the house, and his dad sprawled in a lawn chair watching him, drinking a beer, telling Walt to keep his elbows in. To stop shooting like he was scared of the basket.

It was just a day. A Sunday. A nothing, no big deal, who cares if you miss this shot day.

It was enough to brace his rolling stomach.

He gave the ball one more hard bounce against the floor. He lined up his shot, flexed his fingers, and launched the ball.

He watched that ball, willing it, wishing it, into the basket.

It hit the rim, bounced once, rolled right.

The gym went quiet, hushed, someone yelled, "Go in!"

And it did.

The crowd went berserk—tie game.

Again the hand claps and butt smacks, and the ref blowing his whistle and then the ball was back in his hands.

Walt dribbled twice. Blew out all his breath. Wiped the sweat off his face with his arm, which didn't help much, but he was stalling for time. He couldn't quite hold onto the fantasy. The *it's a normal day* fantasy. He kept seeing MaryAnn Arneson out of the corner of his eye, clutching her pompons to her chest and looking like her whole world hinged on this basket, and that got him to thinking about other people. Al. Mr. Kerestes. Their worlds rested on this basket, too.

Not Dad though. Dad was the same whether it was Sunday or the ftate Finals. Dad would be a mean old cuss, either way.

Do it again, you baby.

He didn't even line up the shot, he just wildly threw it in the air, sending with it every hope and wish and daydream he had ever had in his seventeen years. His mom was here, his father watched, and it might just be the best moment of his life. Or the worst. And now, with the ball in the air, it wasn't anything he could control anymore.

The ball hit the backboard, the front of the rim, and fell in.

The screaming deafened him and he couldn't stop laughing. There were bubbles in his veins, making him light as air. He was air, he was lifted up, and when he looked down at Al and Bear he couldn't believe it.

"Holy shit!" he screamed.

"You're telling me!" Al screamed back.

He was being carried away on the shoulders of his team. A champion. He had done it. He twisted, looking behind him, searching out the worried hen in a blue dress and an old man who might be smiling.

His mom stood beside an empty chair and her face said she was sorry.

His dad missed it. Walt's glittery gold champion feeling crashed to the ground.

"Good job, son!" Mr. Kerestes yelled and clapped a hand on Walt's knee, and Walt smiled and told himself it didn't matter. So what if the old man didn't see it?

So what?

8

W alter felt like he was fading. Slowly seeping out of himself from some unknown wound. The boys and the crowd slowly disappeared like phantoms, losing their outlines and then their ghostly shapes. The noise echoed, diminished, and then slid into silence.

And then there was a loud *pop!* and Walter sat in the stands again, clutching his ears.

My God, those samples are potent things. Like being in a movie or something.

Walter grinned and slapped his knee. What a day. What a day that had been. He could remember exactly what it felt like to be lifted on those shoulders, like some part of his flesh and bone was still up there. Over the years the victory had faded until all he remembered was his father not being there. One more cross for this father's memory to bear. It was nice to remember what that day had really been about. Winning the game. Being carried off the court on Al Torreno's shoulders.

"Hey, that was..."

He turned, looking for Peter, and found his mother up in the stands alone.

Is this the past? Present? Is she a ghost? Am I?

He decided he didn't care. It was his mother there; a blue beacon among the brown stadium seats. She stared after where the boys had gone into the locker rooms. Her fingertips pressed to her lips and tears were on her cheeks.

She hiccupped, part laugh, part sob, and collapsed into her chair like her bones had liquefied all at once.

Walter took the stairs two at a time to his mother's side.

Paulina Zawislak was not an attractive woman. But she smelled like sugar and sauerkraut, and she had tried to balance her husband's unpredictable anger and constant discontent with a steady never-ending stream of hot tea with sugar and brandy.

She pulled a handkerchief from the pocket of her blue dress and lifted her glasses to wipe her eyes. She laughed while she did it and Walter felt the tidal flow of his pride and a sudden mourning for his mother.

"Hey Mom," he breathed. He stretched an arm across the back of her seat and studied the plump firm peachiness of her face. He breathed deep the smell of vinegar and baking that had settled into her pores and become, in his memory, the distinct fragrance of motherly love.

Finally, she rested her hands in her lap, her fingers tugging at the lace she had stitched. She smiled.

"Did you see our boy?" she called out, and Walter whirled to see his father standing at center court, looking toward the locker room where the voices of the team could still be heard. There was a particularly loud yelp and Walter remembered the icy blast of water from the shower they had thrown him into.

Vicktor Zawislak punched his beat-up fedora onto his

thinning white hair and turned, his hands tucked into the navy work pants he wore every day, including the day he died.

"I sure did," he said. "I sure as hell did."

"Where'd you go?" Paulina asked, and Walter heard himself seconding the question.

"Yeah, where the hell did you go? I looked for you!" Walter was on his feet before he even knew it. He ran down the steps to his father before his slow, lumbering heart could beat twice.

"That was pretty tense." Vicktor shook his head, his attention still on the closed locker room door. "I needed a little room to pace." His white mustache twitched.

My God, he's smiling.

"So you saw it? Walt looked up here and when he didn't see you..."

"Of course I saw it," Vicktor announced like he was Father of the Year and the question insulted his devoted parenting. "I was right over there." He pointed with his thumb to the dark corners by the doors.

Walter felt years of righteous anger and indignation burn and smoke in his chest.

"You have got to be kidding me."

"Didn't think the shit had it in him," Vicktor muttered and sucked on his teeth. "Let's go, Paully girl," he called out, using a nickname for Paulina that Walter only heard on his folks' anniversary or the rare Sunday mornings after his father had done well at the Saturday night poker game. Walter's mother stood from her chair, her coat and purse over her plump arm.

She put that arm around Vicktor's waist and the two of them walked out the door. Vicktor even bent to kiss his wife's golden hair.

"I'll be damned. I thought the bastard missed it," Walter breathed.

"I know," Peter said.

"He never told me he saw the game!"

"Did you ever ask?"

"Are you kidding?" Walter laughed bitterly. "I never asked that man anything, ever. Do you know the shit he put me through?" Walt faced Peter, who was standing next to the green filing cabinet that had ripped a hole in the pale gold boards of the basketball court.

"Some of it." Peter's nimble fingers flipped through his files.

"Nothing was ever good enough for that asshole." Walter was getting mad all over again, like the game was yesterday. Like the daily slices and slashes at his ego and pride were still going on and home was never a safe place.

"I don't know what he wanted from me, but man I could never give it. I worked with him for two years after I graduated. We nearly killed each other. He always said that I didn't know what it was to be a man—he told me that when I was six." Walter rolled his eyes at Peter who didn't laugh. "But when I enlisted—" He put his hands in his pockets and studied the conference banners that hung from the ceiling. "Well, things were different."

"Things are not always what they seem, Walter."

Walter looked around the old auditorium, the seats. In particular, the empty one of his father's that loomed so large in his memory. "I can't believe he saw it."

"He saw it twice." Peter tucked the file back in the green cabinet and the thing retreated into the ground and the wood healed itself.

"What do you mean, twice?"

The boy's eyes glowed again and he grew taller as Walter watched, his throat dry, his throat aching.

"When your dad died, this was his day. This was the day your father relived, Walter."

Walter's legs gave out and he collapsed into the brown auditorium chair.

"Son of a bitch," he muttered.

Peter stood up from where he had been sitting next to Walter in the gymnasium. A ball appeared in his ghostly hands and Peter started practicing free throws.

He was terrible, Walter noticed. The kid threw too hard and from his palms, not the tips of his fingers.

But he hit every basket.

They had been there a long time and already Walter's memory was erasing the details of the day. The roof was vanishing in chunks and grass was growing up between the boards in the court. The net hung in tatters from the rim.

"What day did my mother relive?" he asked, wanting suddenly to have her thick arms around him again, like he was a boy and brandy tea would make all this go away.

"What day do you think she relived?" Peter asked, deking and ducking past imaginary point guards and forwards.

Walter looked up at the ceiling, where the wooden and metal beams were fading to dust and patches of sunlight came through, like high beams, to touch the floor, illuminating the maple's slow dissolve into the ether. "The day Christopher came home from the hospital," he guessed. It had been the only time all four of them had lain in his parent's big bed with all the pillows and mystery of adult sleeping arrangements.

Peter stopped his fantasy game and stared at him, smiling sadly.

"You know I've been doing this for a few years. And I've learned some things."

"Does this have anything to do with my mom?"

"Girls grow up to give their mothers grief," Peter said, ignoring Walter. "Because they see their mothers as humans. With faults and problems and prejudices and silent secret wants. Little boys never see their mothers as they really are. Mothers are perfect—simple. Living only for them. And those little boys grow into men who never see their mothers as they really are."

"I doubt my mother's waters ran very deep," Walter said. "It's the sort of thing my father would put an end to."

Peter pulled his phone from his belt and tapped away, shaking his head at Walter all the while.

"Your mother relived the day she, your father, and her parents left Poland." Peter's eyes glittered with a certain unappealing satisfaction. Smarmy bastard. "It was their wedding day."

Walter was surprised. Oddly wounded.

"Hey, you've got a decision to make. How about it?" Peter asked, dragging Walter from his hurt feelings. "Is this the day? Basketball champ? It's a good one. All the running, all that glory, you looked good up on their shoulders." The boy dribbled and put a layup in the crumbling basket. The ball disappeared in a poof of smoke.

This wasn't the day, but Walter wasn't sure he wanted to

leave just yet. Lingering here in this old memory felt good. Made him happy in a sad way.

"I'm sure the night was probably just as good." Peter shrugged. "A few parties..."

Walter surged to his feet. He remembered what had happened that night. How could he possibly forget *that* night? The maudlin nostalgia lifted from around his shoulders and he smiled.

"Great, so if you want to just sign the..." The contract suddenly appeared in the kid's hands and he pulled a pen from behind his ear.

"I don't want to relive it, I just want to see something."

"Oh." The boy was hesitant and Walter was ready to beg. This had been a *very* big night for him. "I don't know, I've got..." The boy looked down at the small pager on his belt. "Well, would you look at that. She had the chicken." The contract and pen vanished. "Where to?"

"Give me twenty minutes around midnight."

The kid clouded over, there was a spark and flash, and they left the auditorium and memories of his father behind.

WALTER AND PETER sat on a stone fence watching a 1961 Buick Skylark. Walter plunged his hand into a drift of snow next to him on the fence. It was painfully cold for about three seconds and then the feeling faded out. Not to numbness, but to nothing. He didn't feel the wet or the cold.

Weird.

"I'm starving," Walter groaned, pulling his hand out of the snow. "Aren't you hungry? Or don't you eat?"

"Don't eat, but I imagine if you just tell yourself you're not hungry you won't be hungry."

"I'd rather tell myself I was eating popcorn," Walter mumbled. The kid tore his gaze away from the lights of Beaverton, which twinkled below them in all of their grid-pattern beauty, except for the Exxon sign that glowed with a neon beauty all its own on the south side of town. Peter's eyelashes twitched and a paper cone filled with popcorn from the Hub Theater, which was somewhere in that grid of lights, appeared in Walter's hand.

"There you go," Peter said.

"Thanks, kid." With real glee Walter tossed a kernel of corn into his mouth. The salty fat deliciousness touched his tongue and then vanished. He crammed a handful into his mouth and it was the same thing—a taste, the familiar squeeze and gush of his tastebuds, and then nothing. It was a bitter tease. "Thanks a lot."

"You're dead." Peter shrugged. "What do you want from me?" Peter turned back to the lights of the town. "It's pretty up here."

Walter had never noticed, but Make-out Rock did have a sort of picturesque quality to it that had nothing to do with trying to get to second base with a girl. It was dark and private, and the rolling lowlands of southern Wisconsin were an ebony sea before them, gilded in elevated places with the illuminated specters of far-off towns.

"It's gonna get prettier." Walter grinned, feeling like the hormone-riddled seventeen-year-old boy who'd won that state championship.

The windows of the '61 Skylark were getting pretty steamy.

The boy checked his pager again.

"I thought the woman chose chicken?" Walter asked.

"She did, but I've got my eye on a guy who has been

drinking and is looking for his keys." The kid nodded and then smiled at Walter. "He called a cab."

"I thought all of this was planned out—"

Peter scoffed.

"It's not?"

"No way." Peter crossed his legs and fiddled with the crease at his knee. "Every person is born with general decency. We miss some—Manson, Hitler, Dahmer. But for the most part you all get a sense of right and wrong at birth. But what you do with it is constantly surprising." Peter gave Walter the hairy eyeball. "You people should know better by now. But..." He heaved a dramatic sigh. "That's life. Literally."

Walter let that little insight sink in like a rock. "There's no plan?"

"There's faith, Walter. That's all. Faith on every side of the coin, from every angle, it just comes down to—"

A loud squeal and some shrieking laughter pealed out of the Buick.

"Kid, hold that thought."

Walter grinned and the Skylark shimmied and shook and the screaming laughter got louder.

"Any minute now..."

The back door flew open and MaryAnn Arneson fell out into the grass and snow, laughing her head off and wearing—oh dear God—nothing but her cheerleading skirt.

Rosie was the love of his life, the most perfect woman in the world. But MaryAnn Arneson had a pair of tits that he used to dream about.

MaryAnn picked herself off the ground, her pale skin glowed in the moonlight and those breasts, high and round and young, bobbed slightly as she stood.

"Amen," Walter breathed, so pleased that those mythical breasts were better, more perfect than he remembered.

An arm, his own, seventeen-year-old arm reached out from the car and grabbed her hand.

"I don't know, Walt," she said, all the laughter and giddiness gone, and now she just looked like a young woman, a girl really, standing at the edge of adulthood. Walter felt her innocence all over again, but sharper, more real and fragile than he could have even comprehended at seventeen. It was beautiful and humbling the trust she had put in him that night.

"I'll stop, sweetheart. Just say the word and I'll stop." Walter's young voice cracked. He'd meant it. He actually remembered, despite all his hormones, that part of him hoped she would say stop. He had been a scared virgin, too.

"Promise?" Her hand fluttered over her chest like she was crossing her heart and Walter felt the sudden bite of tears. *Don't do this*, he wanted to say. *Be a child a little longer. Don't let go of this guilelessness.*

"Of course, of course I promise," the young him panted.

"Okay," she breathed.

MaryAnn crawled back inside and the laughter turned to low moans.

"Do you want me to stop?" his voice asked.

"No, Walter. No. It's okay."

"You sure?"

"I'm sure."

"Because I can—"

"Walter!"

There was a quick pained gasp. A deep groan.

Walter stood and looked away from the car, at the lights of the town. The memory was altered from this perspective, tainted by age and knowing better and filled with a wistful wish that perhaps he had held on to childhood a little longer.

Because things were never so simple and sweet again.

"I want to go," he said.

His own youth left a bitter taste in his mouth.

10

I n the little girl's backyard the sun burned off the clouds and steam drifted up from the earth.

Walter lurched and collided with a swing, the earth unanchored and fluid in the moments just after arrival in this backyard after leaving the escarpment.

The pain radiated through his body like he'd been hit with a sledgehammer.

"Uh, God," he moaned and belched up the bubble of nausea.

Walter rolled over to his side, trying to remember Rosie's Lamaze breathing lessons.

It was getting harder. Peter had been right about that.

The girl had taken off her pink raincoat in order to slide down her plastic slide and right into a puddle that had formed at the bottom. She landed, pink boots first, and mud, water, and pine needles sprayed heavenward and a rainbow appeared in the wet air around the girl's poofy pigtails.

Peter applauded the girl's spectacular splash landing and she threw her arms over her head. For a second Walter thought maybe the girl could hear him.

"Her mother is going to kill her," Peter said. The little girl ran right through him to climb back up the slide.

For a moment, while her flesh and bone passed through the air and glitter of his phantom shape, it seemed to Walter's untrustworthy eyes that Peter glowed bright.

"Beth!" A woman, tall and thin and mad, stood at the sliding glass door, her hands fisted on her hips. "What in the world do you think you are doing?"

"Told you." Peter smiled and sat at the top of the slide to watch. "This girl never learns. Watch."

"Mom, it's getting hot out," Beth whined, and Walter remembered a day by the lake when Jennifer, about Beth's age, had pushed Rosie's "stay away from the edge of the water" rule until Walter had to go in after her.

"I don't care, you're coming in."

"But Mom..."

"One." The woman's posture became that of a mother not to be messed with. "Two." Beth grabbed her jacket, dragging it through the mud puddle, and clomped up the stairs and in the sliding glass door.

The mother took the tea towel from off her shoulder and swatted her daughter on the butt as she tramped by.

Peter watched until the vertical blinds swayed back into place before looking over at Walter.

"What are we doing here?"

"Where?"

"This yard."

The boy was acting strange. And strange, to a dead man, who'd tried to bring himself back to life and had been traveling willy-nilly through his own past, was really saying something.

"Where would you rather be?" The boy asked, and for a split second the yard and the mist and the smell of pine vanished, and they were in the basement of the Horner Funeral Home in Beaverton, Wisconsin. Walter's body was laid out like a raw turkey on a table and Jay Horner, who used to run track with Walter in high school, was putting socks on Walter's pale, dead feet, humming along with the radio.

Walter cringed at the sudden change and the sweet chemical smell. "You want to keep coming back here?" Peter asked. "Watch yourself get dressed for your funeral?"

"No," Walter said, trying not to breathe through his nose.

"Of course not," Peter nodded. "It's depressing."

And in a flash they were back in the yard, swinging in unison on the little girl's swing set.

"But who are these people?" Walter asked. "I mean, why do we..."

Peter's phone rang and the boy dug his feet into the soft mud to stop his swinging. He checked his phone, nodded grimly, and cast an apologetic look at the sky.

"You still need to pick a day," Peter reminded him, and Walter dug his own feet into the ground.

"Okay," he said, not intending to ever pick a day, but willing to use up whatever time he had available for these fluid trips to the past. "Something else from when I was a kid."

Peter nodded, and from the ground between the slide and door a hulking black metal machine, like an early arcade game, ripped through the earth and Walter recognized the old microfiche machines. The boy leaned down and looked through the viewfinder; his hands on the knobs toggled whatever he was watching on the screen forward.

"High school graduation?" Peter asked.

Walter shook his head. He'd gotten blind drunk and passed out on his front porch.

"Science fair, summer camp, spelling bee—"

"Spelling bee!" Walter grinned. "Not mine, though. Chris's."

"You want to go see your brother win a spelling bee?"

"That night. My mom took us into the city." She'd done that a lot, taken them out for dinners without their dad, but this night she'd been particularly fun. Silly, even. She'd put a straw between her lips and nose and pretended it was a mustache. They'd had ice cream before the meal. She let them share a beer, telling them strong, smart boys deserved such things. Such fun.

All the way home they'd sung the Polish folk songs she'd taught them as babies.

Peter consulted his magic device and nodded in surprising agreement. "Good idea," he said. "But there's something more to that night that you should see."

Peter blinked and Walter was hurled backward, lifted up, and spun. His stomach knotted, his guts twisted. And then—light as a feather—he landed in his parent's bedroom.

MARCH 17, 1955

The night of the Beaverton County Elementary School Spelling Bee

VICKTOR LAY BACK on the bed, his arms over his chest as he watched Paulina get ready for her celebratory dinner with the boys.

"I'm not here," Walter said, looking around his parent's

small bedroom. "I thought you could only show me things I was around for?"

He'd rarely gone into his folks' room. It was like a dragon's inner sanctum when he was a kid. Dad spent a lot of time here, watching the old black and white, stretched out across the bed with a beer.

Walter had never noticed the needlework sunflowers framed in the corner—his mother's handiwork. Or the stack of books by his father's side of the bed. Walter tilted his head to read the titles. Nonfiction, mostly. A couple of Agatha Christie mysteries.

"Usually," Peter said, smiling and twinkling like a boy with a secret. "But I think it's for the greater good to break the rules in this instance."

Wearing his most annoying all-knowing expression, Peter sat down on Walter's parents' bed. He slid up the white chenille bedspread to lean against the cheap pine headboard, next to Vicktor.

Walter—even though he was dead, even though Peter was a ghost or an angel or whatever—Walter was nervous about those black shoes on the bedspread.

That was the power of Vicktor Zawislak.

Peter looked small, ridiculous, like the utter opposite of Walter's father and Walter had to stop himself from warning Peter to stay away from the man. Like his father's anger and bitterness might, across death, infect the boy with something. A cold, maybe. Strep throat.

"I think you're going to be interested in what your parents have to talk about." Peter's black eyes glittered.

"Why can't I go?" Vicktor asked his wife.

Walter's jaw dropped, not just at the request, but at his father's tone. He was whining. Walter and Christopher would have been slapped, called babies, had they used that tone of voice. "I'd like to go into the city. Have a pork chop."

"You wanted to go?" Walter asked his father. "But you never went out with us for these dinners."

"Keep watching," Peter whispered, like they were at a movie.

Mom sat at her vanity table, powdering her face with an aged pink puff. The smell wafted up to Walter—flowery and sweet and undeniably his mother. She wore her one good dress—red sateen with the belt and embroidered collar. It reminded Walter of weddings.

Paulina looked back at her husband's reflection in the mirror, her face soft. Her eyes warm. Loving.

This is what happened in his parent's bedroom? Walter wondered. His father whined and his mother was affectionate to him?

No wonder they rarely let him and Chris in here.

"Come now, *Tata*. You spoil the fun." She clipped on the white pearl earrings she'd said were her mother's. "You make the boys uncomfortable."

Walter braced himself for his father's explosion, even going to far as to step between them. As if his ghostly body would be better protection than his earthly childhood body. But he'd never heard his mother speak to Dad like that. Never even dreamed she was capable of such honesty.

"I am too hard on them," Vicktor said, picking up the beer he had sweating on the bedside table.

"*Tata*." Paulina stood, her solid body wide, stout, and capable. She walked over to the bed where Dad pouted, and braced her hands on his shoulders. She stroked his face. Smiled into his eyes with unflinching affection.

Walter collapsed onto his mother's vanity stool, his knees weak, his perceptions of his parents blown to bits.

"I told you it was good," Peter said.

"You are their father," Paulina practically cooed. "It is your job to make them men."

Vicktor shook his head. "I know, but they don't like me. My own sons. I scare them—"

"They love you," Paulina insisted. "And when they grow they will thank you for what you've done. For the way you have made them strong."

Vicktor nodded, reluctantly, and Paulina leaned down and kissed his forehead.

"Here." Vicktor dug into his blue work pants. "Buy the boys dessert. Ice cream or whatever they've got."

"Thank you, *Tata*." Paulina kissed him again and turned to leave.

"Flip on the set," Dad said, and Paulina hit the button that sparked the old TV to life.

She walked right by Walter and there was no misinterpreting the satisfaction that wreathed her face as she left Vicktor behind.

Walter spun to face Peter.

"See?" Peter crowed. "You don't know your mother as well as you thought."

"She encouraged him," Walter said, flabbergasted. "She —" He couldn't even find the right words for what he'd seen.

"Manipulated him?" Peter supplied. "Not everything is as it seems."

Walter watched his father settle into his place in front of the TV, while the sound of the old Buick starting came in through the open window. Christopher called shotgun.

"I don't get it!" Walter cried. Every betrayal of his childhood doubled and redoubled. It wasn't just his father's cruelty he carried anymore, it was *their* cruelty. "Didn't she see what he was doing to us?"

"Walter—"

"She wanted him to treat us that way? How could a mother do that?"

"Walter, you're getting worked up."

The walls of the room started to smoke. Gold flames with blue hearts that mirrored Walter's wounded memories flickered up the walls, eating the needlepoints and stacks of Agatha Christie novels.

"Of course I'm getting worked up!" he yelled. "Why did you show me this? What was the point? Like this whole thing isn't painful enough? You have to do this to me?"

"Okay." Peter climbed off the bed where Vicktor remained, unaware of the flames, the ruination of Walter's fond memories of his mother. "This was a mistake. I get that. This is why there are rules about these things."

Flames cruised over the ceiling and Peter grabbed his phone.

"Something happy, something happy," he muttered. "Got it." He looked up at Walter, the smarmy expression gone. Regret carving lines into his young face. "I'm so sorry, Walter."

The floor dropped out of his parent's bedroom and they landed in the alley behind that crappy apartment above the liquor store that he'd lived in after the war.

Walt recoiled at the sudden smell of urine and sour booze.

"Walter?" Peter said stepping out from behind the dumpster.

"Why did she want him to treat us that way? All these years I thought she was scared of him. That's why she never stopped him. But she wasn't scared she was..." He tried to find a word to match the satisfaction he'd seen in her eyes, that smile on her lips, but the only word he could think of made him sick. "God, happy? She was *happy* with the way he terrorized us?"

"She's from a different generation. A different place," Peter said. "Different ideas of what it meant to be a man and a father."

"But it's like she didn't want us to like him."

Peter shrugged. "She got all your love that way. She never had to be the bad guy."

Christ, it all made sense. The way she swept onto the scene to comfort them, provide the love he and Christopher never got from their father. The brandy tea, the special nights with just the three of them, the secret treats and gifts.

"Does it really change how you think of your mother?" Peter asked. "Does it diminish the love she gave you? The love you gave her?"

Walter tried to hold onto his anger. Pack all of his injured feelings into hard balls of ice and stack them with the rest of his grudges. But he couldn't hold onto his righteousness and surprise; they melted away even as he tried to hold on to them. Was it because he was dead? Was it because he made his own mess of parenting? Did it even matter why forgiveness should come the way it did?

He shook his head. "I guess not."

Peter's fingers flew over his phone and he finally nodded. "You know your mother didn't make him that way? Vicktor Zawislak was a son of bitch, no matter what. And your mom just figured out how to work him. She figured out how to make your home livable."

"How do you know that?" Peter asked, grasping onto the straw Peter held out to him. A way to keep his memories intact.

Peter held up the device. "Your father was a born bully."

The sun was coming up over the edge of the concrete

buildings, turning the sky the color of orange sherbet. A million years ago this used to be his favorite time of day. A side effect from the years of fishing.

"Do you want to go back to that celebration dinner with your mom and Christopher?" Peter asked, a cowed puppy at his side.

"It's okay," Walter said. "I'm glad I saw that. I'm glad...I'm glad I have a better picture of my dad. My mom."

Peter eyed him carefully. "Perhaps we're seeing some progress here."

A breeze blew the smell of sour trash toward them.

"What the hell are we doing here?" he asked.

Peter pointed over Walter's head and he turned in time to see the back door of his apartment open and Walter, young and trim in those years after the war, stomp down the metal fire escape with a garbage bag in his hand.

He skirted the puddle of urine and the vomit and lifted the black metal lid of the green dumpster. He tossed the bag inside and at the sound of shattering glass Walter remembered this day.

"My first sober sunrise after the war," he said, watching himself dust off his hands. Young Walt turned to go back to the apartment, but caught sight of the pink sky on the eastern horizon.

He tucked his hands in his pockets and watched the sky brighten, pale pink turning florescent, turning orange. Finally the giant blazing sun burned through the clouds and the day began.

"It was after our first date," Walter said, remembering it with awful clarity. Bittersweet perfection.

He and Rosie'd talked into the wee hours. He'd drunk ten cups of undoctored coffee and now he couldn't sleep. At dawn he'd gathered his bottles and thrown them away.

Walter looked at that young man and remembered the road ahead of him. The things he would face. That sober young man didn't know how to make breakfast or how to dress for work without a slight buzz on. He didn't know where things were, how to talk to people, who to be, and he felt raw like a snake in new skin.

But watching this sunrise he'd been ready to give it a shot. Rosie had given him that. The courage to be better than he was. Faith without proof in the face of terrible obstacles.

Walter followed himself up the stairs. Inside the crappy apartment, his young self took one of the empty coffee cans he'd never gotten around to throwing away off the top of the fridge and rinsed it out.

Hazy new sunlight streamed through the dirty window over the sink, illuminating his face, the scar on his neck, the tiny bit of hope his smile carried in the corner of his mouth.

He dried the can, took out his wallet, counted three singles, and dropped them in the can. He grabbed the loose coins in his pocket, shook out eighty-one cents, and dropped the change in after the bills, the pennies and nickels clanging and clattering against the tin.

Three dollars and eighty-one cents. The price of a bottle of Ol' Granddad.

"You ready to go?" Peter asked, standing in the open door.

"The pain will stop?" Walter asked, hopeful. He was getting pretty sick of the whirlwind effect of going in and out of these days.

"That's up to you, Walter." Peter consulted his pager. "Well," he said after a moment. "I totally forgot about that."

"What?"

From the cracked linoleum in front of the sink popped

another door. This one serge green canvas, held together
with duct tape and flimsy one-by-two pine slats. A hot and
moist wind blew through the screen and licked Walter's
face. He closed his eyes in sudden recognition. There was
only one place where the wind felt like a dirty washcloth.

I don't want to go in there.

He thought he said it. He meant to. He meant to scream
it but instead he reached out a hand and touched the rusted
spring coil that kept the door from flapping in the wind.
This night was something he'd done his best to forget—he'd
pushed it down, sunk it under gallons of alcohol, lost it in
drugs and neglect and yet...here it was, like it had always
been, just on the other side of something, waiting like an
animal for someone to open its cage.

"You know it's always a pleasure when we get one of
you."

"One of me what?" Walter whispered. He touched the
canvas—slightly damp from the humidity

"A war hero."

Walter pushed open the door and entered hell.

HE'D BEEN HERE ONCE. This patch of jungle on the edge of a
swamp. A million years ago for five hours. Five hours that
had stretched like a millennia—endless and all-encom-
passing.

They'd been in the field two days and were humping
back to rendezvous with their replacements.

It was silent among the dark palms and mangroves. No
sound. No stars. Not even a breeze rustled the elephant
grass. Just black silence and that was a very bad thing.

"Some of our war heroes choose the day that made
them heroes," Peter said, appearing beside Walter in a

helmet and flack jacket over the dress pants and shirt he wore.

The jacket and the helmet fit the kid, but it still looked so wrong. He looked like all the fresh meat he'd seen in his tour of duty—ridiculous and sad, boys playing at being men and scared shitless.

Walter walked on, his internal compass leading him deeper into the heat and the endless dark. To that place— that divot in the earth, the mangrove with all the leaves shot off—where everything had changed.

It had been a standard search and destroy mission. Creeping through the jungle, knee deep in the muck and mud, their hearts hurtling into their throats at every noise, their fingers, already jumpy, ready on the triggers of their M-16s.

But the noises they heard were always their own.

Charlie was a quiet son of a bitch.

At this time, Walter'd had three months left on his second tour and had been thinking about home as a series of sensations. Cool sheets. Ice. Dark movie theaters. When he tried to imagine himself there, with his mother, drinking her brandy tea, he got lost. He couldn't find himself on the chair or the couch, in front of the TV. He could see the river up at his grandparent's cabin—but he couldn't place himself next to it. Not anymore. Sex with MaryAnn Arneson was a skin flick. He'd done it—could probably do it again when he got home, he could imagine those breasts, see those ivory legs, the dark brown curls—but he didn't feel it.

All those memories were there, he just was never in them.

It was like the popcorn the kid had given him at Make-out Rock—there, but not there, both at the same time.

"You're my first, you know," Peter said. "I get some of the

guys that died in battle, but you're the first decorated surviving war hero I've managed."

"Is that what you're doing?" Walter asked. He stepped into a puddle, remembering how it would suck at his leg like a thousand-pound weight. He pulled up his leg, but in death the mud was no more than air, it didn't even stick to his old loafers or brown pants.

"What?"

"Managing me?"

"Sure."

"You're not doing a very good job."

Up ahead the canopy broke, solid streamers of bright white moonlight slid down into the dense forest, and Walter found himself in that jungle. Twenty-three years old, crouched and tense, looking right for a command from Sarge. Jonesy was on his left and the rest of the patrol was spread out in fan formation on the right behind Sarge among the trees that skirted a rice paddy.

But as bad luck would have it, they were walking right into a unit of Viet Cong.

There was a *snick*, a barely audible vibration against the ear drum, and it could have been anything. A twig. The brush of camos against the vegetation.A suppressed sneeze. But Sarge held up his fist and Walter watched himself stop, and out of some instinct, some beautiful, terrible instinct, get on his belly in the mud behind an elaborate mangrove root system.

He remembered thinking, *Something is out there*. He remembered the way the fear gripped him behind the neck. Paralyzing him.

The swamp breathed—

"I don't want to relive this!" Walter screamed.

And then everything erupted.

11

A

ugust 13, 1968
Mekong Delta, South of Saigon
Vietnam
6th Battalion/31st Infantry, D Company, 9th Infantry
Division

WALTER PRESSED the trigger and applied downward force to the kickback of his rifle. He couldn't see anything but the white-hot sparks of bullets exploding out of the guns a hundred yards in front of him.

He didn't aim. He just fired and got as small as he could in the mud.

Shit. Shit. Shit.

He didn't want to kill anyone, but pulling the trigger and ducking seemed to be the best way to stay alive.

Branches and leaves scattered down in the crossfire, cut to ribbons by the bullets. Something big landed on his back, part of a tree he hoped. The black night turned white and then faded to green only to be lit up again by another burst of gunfire.

Jesus they were close.

The fire slowed and then stopped. Walter smiled and felt the bite of tears behind his eyes—his reaction to the stress was to want to cry. The boys gave him endless shit about it, none worse than what he gave himself.

And then Walter heard it.

"I'm hit!"

Disoriented and with his ears ringing, Walter looked left. Jonesy, the newest guy on the squad, the one most likely to do something stupid that would get him hit, looked back at him wide-eyed but gave him the thumbs-up. He was fine.

Right of him were Sarge and the rest...

A hand came up, reaching blindly out of the vegetation, twenty yards in front of him.

"Oh, Jesus. God. I'm hit."

It was Sarge.

Walter pressed his head down against a root until the lip of his helmet bit into his skull. *What the hell am I supposed to do? Crawl out into the crossfire?*

Sarge was on his second tour—he wasn't fresh meat, and creeping forward into the crossfire was a rookie mistake.

Walter could feel the silence coming from the bank of trees a hundred yards away like a fist in his gut. The Viet Cong were still out there. They weren't going anywhere.

"Help!" Sarge screamed. "Oh God. Help me."

"Quiet, Sarge!" Walter shouted, and the other side of the forest lit up like a Christmas tree, everything aimed right at him.

He hunkered down, hands on his helmet, belly in the mud.

Some of the bullets were so close he could feel their hot breath against his body.

The fire stopped and it was quiet again. Except for Sarge.

"It's my stomach!" he yelled. "Oh my god...the blood."

A stomach wound. Walter inhaled, smelled his own piss, his fear and frailty, and exhaled.

We're all gonna die. They've got us pinned.

He looked right again and Sarge was trying to move. Trying to crawl on his side back to their line—like it was any safer.

"Stay the fuck down!" he hissed, and the bullets thunked and thudded into the tree he was hiding beneath.

They weren't shooting at Sarge. He was already dead in their eyes. Sarge was bait and Charlie was holding out for someone else.

Charlie was quiet and he was really patient.

There was a rustle to his left. Jonesy was backing up through the elephant grass, going for home. Walt signaled him to stay put, but the fear was in the kid's eyes. He looked like one of the scrawny wolves Dad trapped up at the cabin in the winter. Wild and hurt but mostly dead anyway—he just didn't know it yet.

Jonesy wouldn't stay put for anyone. Not Sarge. Not Walt. Not even his momma if she were out there. Like the wolves, he'd chew his leg off to get away.

He belly-crawled backward out of Walt's line of sight.

For all he knew the rest of the guys were doing the same. He couldn't see anyone else in the dark and it seemed like not even the air moved.

"Help!" Sarge whimpered. "Please help me."

Time moved on like a glacier. He couldn't tell if it was seconds or years. He could go with Jonesy. With the rest of the guys. Take his chances on retreat and leave Sarge, who was gut shot anyway, probably wouldn't make it through the night no matter what.

Something clattered to his left. Jonesy, unused to his equipment, stood up and the barrel of his rifle hit his flack jacket and the enemy line lit up again. A rainshower of fire and falling leaves.

The bullets hitting Jonesy didn't sound much different than those bullets hitting the trees. But Jonesy screamed. Once. Like a dog when his paw gets stepped on. And then it was silent.

There was no retreat.

"We're all gonna die!" Sarge cried. Walter was surprised at what the pain was turning Sarge into. It was rumored that Sarge had been shot four times. Walt believed it. He'd seen some of the scars once when Walt had taken a bet from the guys and spied on him in his tent.

If Sarge, on his second tour, as crazy as they come, thought they were all going to die, what chance did they have?

Walter lay in his own urine, his face pressed to the mud and tried to remember something good.

All the states that began with the letter A.

All the countries that began with the letter C.

He didn't know what he was waiting for. More shots from Charlie. Morning. Sarge to die.

"Walt," Sarge called, his voice weaker.

Walt pressed his head hard against the ground. *Please God. Sarge. Just go. Just die. Let us leave here.*

"Walt. I want my mom," Sarge sobbed, sounding as if spit and snot and probably blood were thick in the man's throat. "I want my mom."

Out of the inky darkness to his right, Marcus cried, "Shut up for the love of God!" And there was a flurry of fire that sent Walt scrambling for cover.

Walt tried to block out the screams. Time was a weight pressing on his back, pushing him through the earth until his mouth filled with swamp water and dirt and he couldn't breathe, couldn't think.

"Please, Momma!"

The jungle, the war, Charlie—they were trying to eat him alive. He had to clamp a hand over his mouth so he wouldn't start screaming prayers to his own mother.

And suddenly, before his brain just ate itself and he went running into the arms of the enemy and the sweet hereafter, he realized what he had to do.

I have to get Sarge.

He had to get him and drag him back to the rendezvous point. It was either that or lose his mind. Or maybe he had lost his mind, because anything, even dying, was better than the current FUBAR situation.

He eased out from behind the tree, up the small slope he'd been hiding behind, a climb that felt like Kilimanjaro, like he was naked on Kilimanjaro and thirty men with guns and hate were watching him. He stopped when his foot cleared the last root and took a breath, and then crawled through the muck with the snakes and slugs toward that upthrust hand.

He crawled over one of the branches riddled in the

crossfire, and his camos brushing over the elephant grass
made a rustle so loud he thought farmers in Nebraska could
hear him. He held his breath, waiting for the bullets to rip
into his flesh. But none came. He continued to creep. Slow.
Like when he was turkey hunting with his dad. Dad didn't
use guns on turkeys—said it was a waste of bullets. So they
used to sneak up on them and wring their necks.

Dad. *I want my dad.*

Finally, the mud beneath his belly changed to the wet
metallic soup of spilled blood. He pushed over some
elephant grass and there was Sarge, staring at the sky, blood
bubbling on his lips with every breath.

His hands frantically clutched and pushed at his gut.
Tucking whatever had spilled out of him back where it was
supposed to go.

*Risking my life for a guy who won't even make it through the
night. I really have lost my mind.*

Walter reached out a hand and grabbed Sarge's chin,
forcing his attention from whatever visions had appeared to
him in the night sky. Sarge slowly focused and opened his
mouth, blood oozing like black sludge from the corner of his
lips. Walter put a finger to his own lips and clamped his
hand over Sarge's mouth just to be sure.

One word, one audible breath, and they were both toast.
Sarge nodded, and Walter removed his hand.

He hooked his arm around Sarge's shoulder, getting his
biceps as high as he could in Sarge's armpit, and then he
pulled.

It had to hurt. It must have, Walt could feel Sarge's body
go tight like piano wire. But Sarge didn't say anything.

Walt crawled backward and pulled Sarge nearly sideways.
They were saved, not by any skill Walt had, but by the passing

of a cloud over the moon. The jungle went pitch black, and the grass they displaced in their torturous route back behind Walt's tree to that small cradle of earth couldn't be seen.

Walt picked up speed, splashing in the deep mud, and Charlie could hear that and opened fire, shooting blind into the thick dark—near them, but not at them.

In the chaos and noise Walt got reckless. He lifted himself slightly so he could use his other arm to pull, too. In one giant surge, he lifted Sarge up and over him, onto his own body, and then pushed him, rolling him down the small slope to the safe place behind the tree.

Sarge screamed and the jungle went white. Walt's company lit up, too. Firing back like hell on earth. They hadn't run. He and Sarge were not alone.

Marcus even got up on his knees, peppering the woods with better aim. His mouth was open in a primal scream, but it got lost in all the noise. More screams tore through the night—mostly from the other side.

Walt wondered what kind of foolhardy courage they'd all been sickened with.

He rolled over onto this side and dug his toes into the mud to leverage himself up and over the tree roots. Halfway through his roll, his right leg exploded, just below his hip. Skin, muscle and material from his pants spilt and sprayed his face. His neck burned hot, then cold. The force of the bullet finished his roll and catapulted him toward Sarge. Walt came to rest against Sarge's side, spooned against him like a lover.

We're both dead, Walt thought. He swallowed dense air and the taste of blood. His chest shook with the effort of breathing. He couldn't feel anything below his waist, and slowly all that he could feel—the heat, the mud, the horror and worry he'd lived with for nearly two years—all bled away.

For a second he thought he was on Adelaide Street, playing stickball. Josh Weber had just hit him in the leg with a foul ball.

It's okay, he heard himself say. *It's okay. You did everything you could.*

Believing it, he shut his eyes and let go.

12

W alter sat down next to his dying body.

"It's okay," he told himself, remembering those moments with razor-sharp clarity. The slow stutter and stop of his heart. His lungs. The sudden memory of playing stickball when he was a kid, fighting with Josh Weber about a foul ball.

"It's okay," he repeated. Stroking his own head, covering his already shut eyes like a priest performing last rites. "You did everything you could."

Walter, both the dead one and the dying one, flickered, like the picture on an old black- and-white TV. Walter's brown polyester pants and yellow work shirt vanished, and both Walters wore the blood-stained and filthy camouflage.

Young Walter gasped for breath, his eyes popped open, and the two Walters flickered back.

"It's okay," Walter insisted again, sliding his hand down his own young face until he covered his mouth and nose. "You can let go—"

"Walter!" Peter cried, pulling Walter's hands from their ministrations. "What the hell are you doing?"

From the right, Marcus, his black face gleaming with sweat, charged from the trees. Behind him were Crofty and Bern-dog.

They slung their rifles across their chests, and midstride they grabbed Sarge and Walt by the armpits and hoisted them up.

Walt tried to hold onto his own jacket. Keep himself there. Dying now, while he was young, before he had everything that was taken away from him. Before the agony of what was to come made the bullet wound that had torn apart his leg insignificant.

"You idiot!" Peter yelled, his face glowing white under the helmet. "Are you trying to ruin everything?"

Walter didn't say anything. Like when his daughter had come home that last time, he thought the truth was obvious. He'd already ruined everything.

"You're a hero!" Peter cried. "You saved that guy's life!"

Walter turned eyes that burned on the kid. "December 12, 1969."

Peter blinked. "You want to relive that day?"

"No. Just take us there."

The boy turned his sharp, white nose to the sky and sighed like Walter was testing the very limits of heavenly patience.

"Fine," he said, like Jennifer used to when she was in those ugly, mysterious teenage years.

The jungle spun a quarter turn, but Walter and Peter were still, the world around them clicking and spinning like a cosmic tumbler settling into place. Then the jungle was gone and they were in the crappy one-room apartment Walter had rented above the liquor store when he got discharged from the war.

Walter was passed out on his back, snoring on the

sagging yellow brocade couch handed down from his mother. A bottle, not quite empty, was tipped on its side beside him. The letter, crumpled into a ball, sat in a pool of bourbon.

He still limped, would always limp. They'd removed a lot of muscle in the three surgeries that saved his life. But he'd come home. Decorated and discharged.

Lucky, with just a limp and an addiction to painkillers.

"What's the point of this, Walter?" Peter asked, no helmet, no flack jacket.

"Read that letter." Walter pointed to the ball.

"Really," Peter sighed. "Most of the deaths I manage are not quite so dramatic."

Walter nearly smiled.

Peter grabbed the ball and smoothed out the crinkles.

"Dear Z," Peter looked up, "Z? That's the best nickname someone could come up with?"

Walter shrugged.

Peter rolled his eyes and went back to the letter. "You lucky SOB! How's the leg? Hope it hurts like hell...blah blah bl..." The boy paused and then swallowed, and the air in the room changed with what the boy had read, the knowledge that they both shared. The frenetic energy the boy pulsated with was tranquilized and he started to recrumple the paper.

"Read it."

"Walt—"

"Read the damn letter!"

"I thought you'd want to know" the boy read, "and didn't know if you'd already heard, but Sarge got out of the hospital about two months ago. The belly wound healed up with nothing permanent to keep him from re-upping except for some bad heartburn. Well, you know that crazy asshole signed up for another tour the second he walked out of the hospital. Three days ago he stepped on a land mine while on patrol. Nothing left of him but three teeth and a boot. Sorry, Z. You saved his sorry ass for nothing. Signed, Marcus."

Peter folded the paper and dropped it. The letter fluttered back to the pond of booze like a crippled bird.

"I'm not giving up," Peter said.

"Giving up what?" He was beginning to feel more hollow, emptier. Like he'd been upended and the last of whatever humanity that had been stuck in his corners, clinging to his sides, had finally seeped out. Was he more dead? Or just less alive?

The green shag carpet gave birth to a metal door with safety glass windows. Walter could see the men on the other side past the peeling and faded red stickers that read VFW Post 3878.

"On you," Peter said and pushed open the door. The din of men and band music poured out on a serrated wave of cigarette smoke and recollection.

"You have no idea what you're talking about," he told Peter.

Of his own accord he walked through the door to prove it.

13

I t was like an American flag had exploded in the room. The civilians were wearing red skirts and blue dinner jackets, and Stars and Stripes ties and earrings. Balloons and banners festooned the ceiling and chairs and tables. Red, white, and blue confetti wafted across the cement floor and drifted against table legs every time someone opened a door.

Walter and Peter walked through people, because there was no room to walk around them and Walter could feel the volatile emotions at work underneath the dancing and the small talk. Vietnam wasn't over and even the most patriotic were feeling duped. It was a room full of sad and scared people. But there was nothing the VFW took as seriously as their annual Fourth of July dinner dance.

The high school jazz band was in full swing, wearing Uncle Sam hats and sweating through their navy-blue shirts. The trumpet player had obviously been hitting the spiked punch. The kid was three sheets to the wind and missed half his notes.

But the offbeat trumpet player didn't seem to bother

most of the dancers. And thanks to Rick Ames and his
mickey of hooch there were more dancers than usual. Mr.
Hernandez, principal at the high school, attempted a waltz
with his secretary but they kept stepping on each other's
toes and laughing, while her husband got drunk with the
rest of the vets from Korea.

"Looks like quite a party!" Peter yelled over the noise.

Walter nodded. Quite a party.

"We need something good," Jack Miller, secretary of the
VFW said to two other men standing in line at the bar to get
whiskey sours for their wives. "We need to have some fun
this year."

The three men all cast sideways looks over at the table
shrouded in smoke in the corner.

Ah, Walter thought, both proud and somehow resigned,
there are my people.

He walked through Jack Miller to join them and Jack's
agitation and pity for the guys in the corner clung to Walter
like spiderwebs.

The Vietnam vets sat together—a pack of wild dogs,
their voices like gunfire in the cheerful room. Their grief
and terror paraded across their faces and echoed in their
desperate and manic laughter. And so everyone stayed
away, and the brilliant festivities faded to gray in that
corner.

The air was choked with blue smoke. Thick curls of it
drifted toward the scattered red, white, and blue balloons
that hovered at the ceiling.

The table of men wore uniforms that had been defiled
in a million ways that the World War Two vets always
looked down on. Walter glanced back at the old-timers who
sat along the wall watching the dancers. The old boys had
managed, for the special occasion, to squeeze into their

dress uniforms. Brass buttons strained across beer bellies and barrel chests.

But the boys from Vietnam were gaunt, worn down to sharp edges, and their motley uniforms hung off their bodies like crepe paper the day after a party. One of the only black men in the room turned and Walter staggered for a moment. Oscar Jenkins. Walter had gone through basic training with Oscar and they'd both landed stateside after their second tours around the same time.

Oscar had a marijuana leaf drawn on the back of his camouflage jacket and *make love, not war* printed on the front. He would move to Milwaukee, stop drinking, and find God in about two years. Marry a pretty girl and start some kind of outreach program for homeless vets in the city. Tonight he was in high form, telling the stories Walter had heard a dozen times about the Saigon whore with no legs.

The ladies of the auxiliary picked up their dirty dinner dishes in a hurry and moved off quickly to the quieter men who'd served in Korea.

Walter sat in an empty chair next to the guys and concentrated on the way he remembered cigarettes smelling, and after a while, like a frozen tap thawing, the smell came back to him. Acrid and sharp.

This was familiar. While the basketball game had been a dream, something long ago forgotten, these moments, these landscapes of drink and despair and his exact location in them, were easily recognizable. He was moored here. Any place he got in his life, any distance from this was only measured from this perspective. He was only as happy other places as he'd been unhappy here.

When Jennifer was a little girl and he and Rosie would take her into Milwaukee for the Fourth of July fireworks on the lake, Rosie would tie one end of a piece of red yarn around Jennifer's wrist and then tie the other end around her own. Despite all of their warnings and dire instructions to not wander too far, as soon as he or Rosie let go of her hand, Jennifer would take off running among the crowds. But that stretch of red yarn always brought her up short.

He and Rosie used to laugh, but when he got brought up short after Rosie died he'd known there was a strand of red yarn tied from his wrist back to these years.

He breathed deep, as if going underwater, and the air in this corner of the VFW hall tasted sour, tainted by jungle rot and gangrene. Pieces of these men were dying even as they sat here picking Gloria Poticus's dry pot roast out of their teeth.

"If everyone will take their seats, we will get the program..." Someone up front, Walter couldn't see, tried to clear the dance floor, but nobody listened much.

The president of the Beaverton VFW, Biford Vogler, stood up and made his way to the small stage in the corner. He had a bad hip from a Japanese sniper bullet, but he was one of those soldiers who had not left part of himself on the battlefield, or so it seemed.

There were two kinds of vets, Walter had learned. There was the kind that war added to, made better in some unseen and unknown way. The kind their families and neighbors were proud of and could look in the eye. The other was the kind that war only took away from. Biting out chunks and pieces until there was nothing left but holes.

"Hey, glad you're having a good time. But I need folks to take their seats," Biford said and the crowd on the floor scattered to any available folding chair. "The Ladies' Auxiliary is bringing by some dessert and we got some work to do here tonight."

Peter, whom Walter had actually forgotten about, arrived next to him, consulting his list.

"Why are we here?" Walter asked, watching the white star confetti swirl like a tornado in the draft from the opening door.

His mother stepped into the room and Walter shut his eyes, wishing himself away from this place. This moment.

"This day is on your list. You received a special citation from the VFW for your Purple Heart and Silver Star." Walter opened his eyes and watched Peter scan the crowd, wondering when the kid would catch on. "But I don't see you here."

Biford Vogler took a pair of glasses out of the pocket of his dress blues, unfolded a piece of paper, and spread it out on the podium, rubbing the flat of his hand across the wrinkles.

The crowd was silent, waiting for whatever he might say, prepared to clap and cheer and break into "God Bless America" should Biford require it.

"You're supposed to be here," Peter said.

"I'm here."

"But I don't..."

"I'm out back, getting drunk."

Walter turned, wanting to leave. But he faltered and drifted sideways, like the drunk he had been, into his place in this particular landscape.

14

J uly 4, 1972
   Beaverton Chapter of the Veterans of Foreign
Wars
   14th Annual Fourth of July Dinner/Dance—in
the alley behind the hall

GODDAMN—IT was so hot in Wisconsin in the summer. He'd just spent four years fairly sure that he would never get cool again, that he would just sweat himself into smoke and that would be the end of him, only to come home and be greeted by the same hot, wet air.

No relief.

He tucked his legs up on the edge of the small loading dock and took another swig from the bottle of Ol' Grand-dad. He should go inside. Sooner or later he was supposed to stand up and get some award. Biford had asked him to say a few words about the medals and about Vietnam.

Which was why he was out here sweating to death instead of inside with the loud and cranky air conditioning.

Walt didn't know what to say.

"People were shooting at me. So I shot back." His voice echoed among the trash and brick.

Not much of a speech.

He took another deep swallow of the bourbon, hoping maybe the right words waited at the bottom of the bottle.

He knew Biford wanted him to talk about Sarge but that hardly seemed the talk for a Fourth of July party.

"Someone had to go get him. So I went and got him."

Again, not much of a speech.

Walt yanked off his tie and laughed, because it seemed like someplace in that mess there had to be a joke. He took another pull from the bottle and rested his head against the aluminum door of the loading dock.

The sky was too hazy for stars and there was a nebulous ring around the moon that made it look like it, too, was sweating itself into smoke.

Walt fanned himself with his cap and thought of cooler places.

His grandparents' cabin in Minnesota. They'd gone every year for Christmas when he was a kid. It was cold there at that time of year, the kind of cold that hurt to breathe, that made your lungs ache.

That kind of cold seemed like a myth. He shut his eyes and tried to conjure it up.

At the far end of the alley a cat screeched and ran helter-skelter into a garbage can. Walt turned and watched his brother walk through the thick air toward him.

He should be surprised. He hadn't told his family about this and they weren't much for dinner dances. He *was* surprised, he guessed. He just couldn't feel it in all this heat.

"What are you doing out here?" Christopher asked, yanking off his own tie and putting it in the pocket of his suit. "They just called your name for the award." He stripped off his brown jacket. He had giant sweat rings under his arms. "Jesus, it's hotter than hell."

"I know."

"We looked for you inside, but you weren't there."

Walt didn't answer because it wasn't a question, and frankly, the way his brother always stated the obvious seemed like a painful waste of time.

"Mom came down to see you get that award."

Christopher's gaze struck Walt's and skidded away. That was how his brother looked at him these days, like a hit and run accident. Fleeting, but hard enough to scratch.

"Where is she?" Walt took a swig to wash away the slimy residue of guilt in the back of his throat.

"In the car. I'm taking her home."

"You should come back, after," Walt invited. "Have a drink or something."

Christopher shook his head. "It's just you VFW guys in there now." He shrugged, looked down at the end of the alley like he couldn't wait to leave.

Walt could relate—he couldn't even bring himself to go in the doors.

Christopher hadn't gone to war. He stayed home, thanks to a heart murmur and bad sight in his left eye from an accident with a BB gun when they were kids. Had things gone the other way the day they fought over that gun, it might have been Walt at home, suffering from migraines and taking over the family business like he'd planned to all along.

Not that he would wish Vietnam on his brother. Not at all. But he couldn't look at Christopher without thinking he would have made a good soldier. The heat and bugs would have killed him, though.

Walt raised the bottle of bourbon to his lips with hands that shook.

"You're drinking?" Christopher's face ran with sweat and the reflected light from the street lamp on the other side of the alley. "Mom made the effort to see you get some kind of medal and you're sitting out here getting drunk?"

Walt wiped his damp neck and nodded. That about summed the situation up.

The silence really stretched and Walt wondered if he was supposed to say something, but before he could, Christopher took the two steps over to the loading dock and hitched himself up beside Walt.

"What's in the bottle?" Christopher asked.

"Granddad."

Christopher held out his hand, surprising the hell out of Walt, who had for years before going to war tried to corrupt him with beer.

"You don't drink," he said stupidly, but passed the bourbon to his baby brother.

Christopher took a meager sip and shuddered. Walt felt a sudden broad river of good will, an accord with things that he hadn't felt in a long time. He and his brother were going to sit out here and have a drink.

It was better than getting the damn award.

He toasted the moment and drank.

"It looks like the moon is sweating." He wiped his mouth with the back of his hand and pointed up to the misty sky. But Christopher didn't look up; he watched his feet like they might walk away without him. "Did you see Hernandez in there with—"

"Walt, we need to talk," Christopher interrupted and Walt's bonhomie evaporated and the episode dropped its shiny disguise. They were in a back alley, sitting in God knew what kind of filth. He was pained by his stink and grime, by his unshaved face.

His brother, on the other hand, smelled like Old Spice and gum.

This was no long overdue moment of brotherhood, here in the squalor.

"Everyone's worried about you," Chris said, and Walt nodded. He knew that. He wasn't sure what he could do about it, but he could feel their eyes on him, their concern like a too-heavy blanket. "Mom, Dad..."

"I'm fine," he lied.

Christopher rubbed a hand through his hair and sighed. "Walt, you're drinking so much. I gave you that job—"

"I appreciate it."

"Is that why you show up late?" Christopher asked. "You show up drunk or so hung-over you can't even see straight. You barely work..."

"I do my job," Walt protested, though mostly on principal. His brother was right. He couldn't muster up any deep pleasure or satisfaction about plumbing the new school out on Highway 10. But anything was better than staying home with Mom, who watched him like he was walking wounded, like at any moment he might bleed out all over the carpet.

Apologize. Tell him you'll try harder. That you want the job. Do it before it's too late.

The voice was left over from the years before the war. It's like the seventeen-year-old basketball player was still inside of him, just opening his eyes after having them closed for the past four years.

"We told you that you didn't have to work. We said you could take all the time you needed. No one expects you to be ready to work after what you've..." He tripped over his words and Walt could feel the scar glowing along his carotid artery.

Christopher cleared his throat and looked off into the dark alley. "You don't have to work right now."

"I want to work." That wasn't true. He thought he should work—that it would help him. That work would tell him who he was and what he should do. If he held a wrench and a length of copper pipe, then clearly he was a plumber. That's how simple it should be. But the wrench looked all wrong in his hand.

Sweat ran into his eyes and he wiped his face hard with his arm, abrading the skin with the rough weave of his shirt. He pressed harder with his arm, raking his skin across the broad weave, digging at the sensitive skin near his eyes.

Wanting, a little bit, to bleed.

"Walt," Christopher whispered. "Tell me what I am supposed to do."

Walt laughed.

"This isn't funny, Walt! I'm trying—"

"You remember Minnesota?" Walt interrupted.

"What?"

"Grandma and Grandpa's cabin?"

Christopher paused. Shook his head. "Sure."

"Remember how cold it was there?"

"Yes," Christopher answered into the heat and silence.

"It was nice there, wasn't it?" Walt rested his head on the door and looked up at the sweaty moon. "So cold."

"You...you want to go up there? Take a vacation up there right now? Because you could go. You could take the time, maybe do some fishing."

"I'm not much of a fisherman anymore." Walt heard the slow quiet hiss of disappointment leave his brother.

He wants me gone, he thought and had another drink. The bourbon loosened his notoriously stuck tongue.

"Remember the winter I told you I found that bear?"

Walt rolled his head to look at his brother's clean profile in the lamplight. "You were eight or something?"

"I was ten," Christopher murmured. "You were twelve."

Walt nodded and took another drink. Christopher was right. He was always right about those little details. Age. Who had who for a teacher.

Christopher, after he stopped being such a baby, grew up to be a scientific kind of kid, always taking things apart to see how they worked. The summer before that Christmas with the bear, Dad had caught a frog and helped Christopher dissect it to find the heart and the brain.

Walt had watched, feeling clumsy and left out.

"You must have been pretty bored to believe me about that bear." Walt laughed.

"You were my big brother. I wanted to believe you." Christopher's smile was a thin, tight grimace. "And, yes, I was bored out of my head."

Walt had never expected Christopher to come along that day. There was no bear. He'd expected his brother to say no and then Walt would have told him how cool the dead bear was, how he could see the heart and the lungs, and too bad that Christopher was such a baby that he didn't want to go.

But Christopher said yes and started putting on his boots, and Walt'd had no punch line for the lie. No final trick that would fulfill his desire as a big brother to torture his little brother. So Walt just led his brother out into the woods and waited for something to come to him.

"I got so panicked." Walt looked at his hands and watched them shake. "The longer we walked, the more sure I was that I got us lost."

"You kept walking though." Christopher's laugh was the first easy sound between them. "We broke through the ice on that stream and you fell into that snow bank and I had to pull you out. But you kept going." His brother said it like it was something honorable.

"Yeah," Walt said on a small huff of air. "I don't know why I did that."

It had started to get dark and cold. And the longer they'd walked the surer Walt had been that they were going to die.

"How long you figure we walked for?" Walt asked.

Christopher shrugged. "A few hours, at least, before I stopped at that stream. Who knows how long you would have gone."

Once Walt had realized that Christopher wasn't behind him anymore, he ran back to find his brother sitting on a rock next to the last stream they had crossed.

"There's no bear, is there?" Christopher had asked, in that serious way of his that was so strange from a ten-year-old. Walt could only shake his head, near tears with worry and embarrassment.

"I think we're lost," Walt had finally admitted.

But his baby brother had just scowled at Walt, the first in a long line of scowls, a thick history of distrust and worry, and a pity that settled between them like fine dust.

"You knew exactly what to do," Walt said. "I was crying and scared, and you just turned around and followed our tracks in the snow back to the cabin."

"It wasn't that big a deal, Walt. You always make those things into big deals." Christopher grabbed the bottle and took a long drink, like a man suddenly dying for the taste of cheap bourbon.

Walt, surrounded by heat and the smell of garbage, peered into the darkness of the alley and couldn't see his tracks.

He had gotten here and now he couldn't get his bearings. Couldn't find home.

Oh God, Chris, please help me. I'm lost.

Christopher put down the bottle and leaped off the loading dock. He swept the grime from his brown pants. "I am really sorry for whatever happened to you over there—" Christopher's voice cracked. "This war...it's terrible. I know—"

From nowhere, or perhaps from those places in his memory and gut that he was trying to drown with bourbon, Walt started to laugh.

He howled until tears gathered in the corners of his eyes and ran down his face like beads of sweat. He held his stomach and accidentally knocked the bottle of Granddad off the landing. It shattered into a million pieces and Christopher swore and jumped out of the way, but was still sprayed with the cheap liquor.

The laughs were giant hiccups, like someone was yanking on his diaphragm, trying to pull out something stuck there in his gut.

"What do you know, Christopher? Huh?" Walt wiped away the tears, but they kept coming faster.

"What do you want me to say, Walt? If you keep drinking like this, I can't keep you on the job. You're a liability."

"I'm a war hero," Walt whispered.

"I know," Christopher said, his eyes wet. "And it's breaking our hearts."

15

Walter's knees buckled and he fell backward in the mud and grass of the little girl's—Beth's—backyard. It sure as hell wasn't the alley with all the broken glass and shame.

"Well, that wasn't quite what I had in mind," Peter said from somewhere behind Walter.

"No shit."

Walter closed his eyes until the world stopped spinning. Until he stopped seeing the look on his brother's face.

"It's mind over matter, Walter, with the dizziness."

Walter lifted his head and searched out the boy. He was sitting cross-legged on the porch beside Beth, watching her industriously braid a doll's yellow yarn hair. He was in a sea of pink plastic and blond yarn.

"Well, maybe if I wasn't being jerked in and out of these damn days, my mind could get used to it."

"Maybe." Behind his glasses, the boy's eyebrows nearly skyrocketed off his head. "If you wouldn't make a mockery out of the days that are supposed to be good memories, I wouldn't have to jerk you around. Seriously, you were getting an award!"

"You sound like my old man." Walter groaned and rolled to his side, the nausea gone, but the shame lingering like grease.

The boy muttered something about not blaming the old man, but Walter ignored him. The novelty of this little adventure had worn off. It wasn't going to be all basketball games and MaryAnn Arneson's breasts. Every day that boy had in his computer was going to be some day Walter had messed up.

The boy grabbed his pager and Walter sighed, resting his head in the mud, wondering who he needed to talk to, or pay, or beg to get out of this mess.

"I'm going to have to move you up a level."

"Level?"

"You were considered an easy file. Statistically, men like you either go back and relive your war hero day or the day they married their soul mate."

Walter closed his eyes, denying both days.

"I've got people piling up out in that hallway," Peter groused. "I need more time."

"I'm not stopping you!" Walter cried. "Let me go so you can get back to work!"

"I'm not going over this with you again, Walter." If looks could kill, Walter would have been...well, more dead. Skewered to the ground perhaps. "There." The kid tapped one more button, slid his fancy machine back into his pocket, and grinned like the smug little prick he was turning out to be. "You are now considered a special case."

"Good for me," Walter muttered, flopping back in the mud. The sky was the bluest thing he'd ever seen. "What do I get?"

"Me."

Walter sat up. Shaken.

It couldn't be.

He turned toward the swing set, searching out the new, terribly familiar voice.

"Over here, Walter."

Walter whirled toward the house and there, standing next to Peter, was his cousin Dan.

"Hello, Walt," Dan said, older and paunchy in a yellow golf shirt and tweed jacket. He pushed open a door to a dark room filled with pink spotlights and a thumping bass line. "Let's go have a drink."

WALT FOLLOWED Dan to a black bar lit up with purple and blue neon.

Topless women danced slowly on top of it.

Walter tried not to stare. Nudie bars were not his kind of place, hadn't been even when he was on the road all those years. Not even when Rosie died. The straightforward commerce of it had just always been too much for him.

"What are we doing here?"

"Not everything is about you, Walt," Dan said. "Hey there, Patty," Dan called to a topless redhead behind the bar. "Two beers and two chasers." He sucked in his gut so he could slide sideways onto his stool. "Have a seat, cuz."

The smoky pink lights picked up the silver in Dan's sideburns, the red spider veins across his nose.

His cousin, forgotten all these years, had gotten old. When Dan turned eighteen he'd hitchhiked to Milwaukee and the family never heard from him again.

And once he was gone, no one even uttered his name.

He'd been a ghost, banished to the attic in old scrap-books kept by Grandma, only coming out in the warnings the adults gave kids on July Fourth. "You could hurt your-self," he'd told Jennifer. "I knew a guy who blew off his whole hand."

"How...ah...how have you been?" Walter asked, sitting on the stool next to him.

"Dead mostly." Dan laughed. He stuck out the belly that strained against his yellow golf shirt and stroked it like a lover. "The good life caught up with me," Dan said.

Patty behind the bar set them up with cocktail napkins.

"Watch this," Dan whispered, the devil in his grin. He put his prosthetic hand on the bar, frozen in a plastic C-grip with a black leather glove slid over top.

"She hates this," Dan whispered.

"Here you go," Patty said, setting the beers and shot glasses down on the bar.

"Be a sweetheart, would you?" Dan asked, lifting his hand just slightly off the black plastic bar. Patty looked at him, expressionless except for the pop and chew of her gum.

"You're kidding me, right?"

Dan shook his head, playing at contrite. "Sorry, doll."

Patty sighed heavily and picked up the pint glass and wedged it, none-too-carefully in the prosthetic's C-grip. It squeaked, and beer sloshed all over the bar and Dan's sleeve.

"Jackass," Patty muttered, just loud enough so Dan could hear and then walked away through the neon lights, turning at once blue then purple.

Dan laughed and lifted his hand with the beer. "Cheers, cuz," he said, clumsily knocking the rim of his glass to Walt's.

"I don't drink." Walt stared at the beaded pint glass.

"I hate to be the one to remind of you the unpleasant reality of your situation, but you are dead. One beer isn't going to kill you." Dan laughed into his pint glass and finished off the second half of his beer.

"What happened to you?"

"You mean when I hitchhiked the hell out of town or when I died?"

Walter shrugged. Either. Both.

"I lived in Mexico for seven years. And then I got a job driving rigs from Mexico City to South Bend, Indiana. Then I started my own company." Dan sighed heavily and braced himself against the bar. "Heart attack at forty." He wiggled his eyebrows at Walt. "I was doing the deed with the most beautiful woman in the world. I came and croaked."

Walt figured his face was about as neon red as the signs behind the bar. He grabbed his beer and took a drink.

The bitter sweetness filled his mouth, gushed over his tongue, across the roof of his mouth and then it was gone.

Another tease.

"The news of my death didn't make it back to the family, huh?" The pint glass squeaked against Dan's prosthetic as he twisted it free. He set it on the bar and tossed back his shot. "Can't say I'm shocked."

Walt spun on his chair and looked out at the empty club filled with strippers but devoid of clients. "Where the hell are we?"

"Heaven."

"You're kidding me," Walt gasped. Surely not. If this was truly heaven, Rosie would be destroyed with disappointment.

"Doesn't fit your idea of heaven?" Dan asked. "You want the strippers to wear wings?"

"I don't have any idea of heaven," Walt said. "But my wife won't be too pleased with this."

"You have no concept of heaven?" Dan asked. "Not even a hope?"

"You're telling me heaven is what you hoped for?" Walter asked, not believing it for a second. "I'm dead Dan, not an idiot."

"Well, if this isn't your idea of heaven, let me introduce you to the Velvet Touch." Dan clapped Walt on the shoulder. "The finest gentleman's club off the Indiana Toll Road." He checked his watch, which was secured around the black-gloved prosthetic. "Sunny's on in about ten minutes so we better make this quick."

"Make what quick?"

"You have to pick a day." Dan signaled Patty for more drinks. And Walter hung his head.

"Do I have to explain this to you, too?"

"No," Dan said. "You don't. You need to stop pretending like your shit was so much worse than anyone else's shit and pick a damn day so Peter can keep doing his job and death can move on."

Walter picked up his shot glass and drank fast in preparation for his second. The whiskey burned the back of his throat for a moment, an old, familiar friend.

"You always were a stubborn son of a bitch." Dan laughed, his big belly heaving for just a second before he took another drink. "You want to know what day I relived?"

Walter nodded.

"The day I died." Dan checked his watch. "I sat out here just like I am now, waiting for Sunny. And just like the day I died, Sunny's gonna come out here in about ten minutes, take off all her clothes, and I am going to fall grossly in love, like I always did, and then I'm going to sneak back to her little dressing room and we're gonna go at it like minks against the sink. But on March 4th, I died." He sighed. "Damn. That was a good day."

"Why that day?"

"Because I was forty years old. Sunny and me had just started dating after months of me trying to get in her pants. My trucking company was finally bringing in some money." He shrugged. "It was all coming around for me. And then it was all taken away from me."

"Weren't you angry?" Walt asked, indignant on his cousin's behalf.

"Pissed!" Dan barked. "Royally pissed." He slammed his fist down for emphasis.

"Keep it quiet!" Patty shouted. "Or I'll have you thrown out!"

Dan chuckled, his massive shoulders heaving like mountains on shifting plates. "You know what's funny? I figured that of all the things I didn't care about anymore by the time I died, the accident was top of the list." He lifted the prosthetic. "It was so long ago I could hardly remember what it was like to have a hand. I barely even thought about it anymore."

"That's good," Walter whispered, wishing he had another beer to wash down the lingering taste of guilt and doubt he had over his father's role in that accident.

"But it was the first thing I made my guy take me to see...can you believe that?" Dan laughed.

"And?"

"And what?"

Walter took a deep breath and shrugged. "Was it an accident?"

Dan looked at him, head-on, but Walter could only stare at his empty glass, watching his cousin from the corner of his eye. It was how the whole family had looked at Dan after the accident.

"Of course it was," Dan said. "Your dad was a mean son of a bitch but he wasn't sadistic. And he felt bad, which was why he treated me the way he did, because the asshole needed some serious counseling, but in the end…"

"You still blamed him?" Walter would have. Walter blamed his dad for dozens of things not nearly as traumatizing.

"Sure." Dan nodded. "But seeing the accident, and the way your dad beat himself up about it, fixed some of that. You've got that chance now, Walt. You can stop blaming Rosie for leaving you and hating her for dying—"

"I don't hate her!" Walt said.

Dan clapped him on the shoulder. "Sure you do, cuz."

"None of this changes anything," Walter said. "Unless your special power is forcing me to pick a day, I think everyone should just let me go."

"That's not my power," Dan said.

"So let's have another drink—"

"But I can let you go back and fix something."

Walter could only blink.

"Something small," Dan said. "But something important."

Walter didn't say anything, silent in the face of such a thing. He sat paralyzed on a bar stool, like he had for so much of his life.

"Patty!" Dan cried and the redhead turned their way. "You mind grabbing the can I gave you earlier?"

Patty popped her gum like her life depended on it and bent to retrieve something from under the counter. She slid a dented, rusted Folger's coffee can across the bar toward them.

Walter felt all things hopeful surge in him, foolishly like a dog longing to chase after cars.

"This is what you get to fix," Dan said. "You get to go back and make this right."

Walter's mouth went dry and he reached out to touch the jagged, rusted lip of the can.

"Why this?" he whispered.

"Because you always said if there was one thing you could do over, you'd make—"

Walter nodded, cutting Dan off. He had said that. A million times. And a million times Rosie had said she didn't care. He'd tried to make up for it with necklaces and earrings, and even a diamond once, and she'd never worn them.

Dan hauled the can to a spot in front of an astonished Walter and gave it a shake. The coins rattled. "The bills are already in your pocket."

Walter reached down and sure enough his empty pocket was now full of cash.

The coffee can was about a quarter filled with seventy-five dollars in pennies and nickels and quarters. Walter knew it down to the odd Canadian penny that had accidentally gotten mixed in.

And the wad in his pocket was a hundred dollars in singles.

He'd saved every one of them, for forty-six clean days.

Walt looked up at Dan, not believing that he was actually going to ask the question of the kid who rolled cigarettes one-handed. "Are you an angel?"

Dan shook his head, the miles of hard road back in his eyes. "I'm your reminder."

Walt swallowed. "Of what?" he whispered.

"That the right thing to do is rarely easy." Dan held out

his prosthetic, the black glove picking up the pink lights. "I missed you after the accident."

Humility and shame choked him. He grabbed Dan's hand to shake it, to beg his forgiveness. But the hand under the glove was real, flesh and bone, and Dan squeezed his palm.

"I'm so sorry, Dan."

Dan held up his hand and the lights dimmed.

"On center stage…" An unseen announcer's voice echoed through the empty club. "Put your hands together for Sunny Day!"

The curtains parted and a tall blond with a little belly and high heels that lit up blue neon strutted onto the stage.

"There she is," Dan sighed. "Ain't she a beauty?"

"Yeah," Walter agreed, looking at the coins in the can. They were the beginning of those years in the middle of his life that didn't seem to belong to him. His fare for a better life. They were Rosie's years.

He didn't know what peace was, really, not without Rosie. And he was very sure that without her he was not capable of it. Maybe he was mad at her; maybe he did blame her for picking him up out of his miserable life only to drop him back into it so suddenly.

He certainly blamed himself for not being what she wanted him to be. Needed him to be.

"You ready?"

Walter looked up to see Peter behind the bar. Luckily, he had his shirt on.

"I really get to fix this?" he asked, cradling the can in his arms. "This isn't some kind of joke? And this isn't the day that I am supposed to relive?"

"Nope."

"Okay," he said to Peter. He stood. "I'm ready."

Like those Fourth of July fireworks that explode, filling the sky with blue phosphorescence and then sizzle and fall like a glittering waterfall back to earth, the bar disintegrated.

Sizzles and pops and explosions of blue and purple neon slowly reoriented themselves into the beige carpet and softly lit glass cases of Meyers Family Jewelers on Main Street in Beaverton.

The last sizzle became classical music tinkling from a small speaker behind the plastic roses on the case.

"Can I help you?" Dale Meyers asked with a discreet half smile, just like he had a million years ago.

16

July 11, 1973
    Meyers Jewelry and Fine Gifts
    Main Street, Beaverton

"SOMETHING SPECIAL?" Dale asked, wiping a hand down his red tie.

Holy mother...Walter couldn't believe it. He was in his young body. Wearing it like a Halloween costume. No glasses. No stomach. His heart...he paused and listened to its hard chug and thump.

He ducked and looked at his reflection in the oval mirror that sat on one of the glass cases.

Hot dog, he thought, stroking his clean-shaven chin. *Look at me.*

No wrinkles. No broken blood vessels. No hanging, jowly flesh.

"Excuse me?" Dale asked. "Are you looking for something special?"

"Yes, I am," Walter said with a big grin. His thoughts from all those years ago played like a staticky radio station in his head. Dim and distorted.

I should have dressed up, the young him thought, eyeing gleaming cases and the carpet that looked like no one had ever walked on it.

Underneath the thrill of being in his young self, he felt shabby and dirty in his work pants and lined flannel shirt. And carrying in a can of change. *Really. What kind of idiot walks into a jewelry store and pays for a ring with pennies?* His thoughts echoed back to him across the distance of years.

The panic and worry and embarrassment he'd been overwhelmed with the first time he'd done this sat like a cherry pit in his throat.

Such wasted emotions. Such stupid selfishness on my part.

He wouldn't make such mistakes again. Not with this gift of a second chance.

Dale Meyers looked like an evening newsman on TV, and Walter liked that about him. Gave this occasion, terrifying as it was, some pomp and circumstance.

Walter's body, still under some control of his younger, headstrong and proud self, stood still, poised to run, every young muscle tight and awkward.

"For someone special?" Dale asked, a gray eyebrow lifted.

Walter smiled.

It's for Rosie. He'd walk into a jewelry store naked on fire for that woman. Something he'd forgotten the first time around.

"I need an engagement ring," he finally said. The words shot out of him like dogs at the track. "Something nice."

"Well," Dale Meyers smiled with charm and understanding, that, even if it was fake or put on, had done the trick and Walter's shoulders relaxed away from his ears. "Luckily, we've got some nice engagement rings, so you came to the right place."

Dale was being so nice to him, Walter felt compelled to get the dirty truth right out there in the open. "I don't have much money." He lifted the coffee can. "One hundred and seventy five dollars."

Dale nodded, wisely. Sagely. Reliving this moment, he saw Dale Meyers for the generous man he was.

"That's all right, son. We can get her something beautiful for that amount."

Walter swallowed and would have done anything Dale Meyers told him to do at that point. If Dale had told him to propose to Rosie with wool socks, Walter would have bought them.

Dale took two steps toward a case in the center of the store. "You can get a diamond, but I'm afraid not a very big one." He pulled out a tray of rings with something called diamond chips in them.

They looked small and unworthy of sitting on Rosie's lovely hand. What was the use of proposing if he didn't have a diamond? Engagement rings were supposed to be diamonds.

"I need to save more money," Walter said.

He felt the urge to run. To take the change down to Rudy's and spill it across the counter and drink himself back to normal.

He quashed it.

"But," Dale said, "if you are perhaps looking for something out of the ordinary for an out-of-the-ordinary woman—"

"Yes," Walter said, nodding his head vigorously,

marveling at how nothing creaked or cracked in his joints. "She's out of the ordinary."

"Well, then, let's look over here."

Dale took another two steps toward a case on the left of the room. More rings. But these had blue stones and green ones the color of grass. Some were blood red.

Dale unlocked the cabinet, reached under the glass, and pulled out a small tray of pearl rings.

Under the jewelry store's fancy lighting, the pearls looked alive and seemed to give off their own special light, a slight pink glow like the skin of Rosie's shoulders.

Walter took a step toward the case and carefully, so as to not get anything dirty or scratched, he placed his Folger's can down on the glass and picked up one of the rings.

A pearl sat in the middle of gold that looked pink in some places and green in others, and was made to look like leaves around the pearl. Like the whole thing was a flower.

"That's very special gold from the Black Hills," Dale said.

Walter had forgotten how beautiful the ring really was. He'd convinced himself that it wasn't all that special, that it was ordinary, in fact. But he could see now that it was perfect.

"It's nice," Walter said. The first time he'd gotten this far, he'd imagined the special gold and the flower pearl on Rosie's finger. He'd imagined himself on one knee, this ring in his hand, tears in Rosie's eyes.

He'd imagined, hoped, and prayed for her whispered *yes*.

It had only been forty-six days. And he'd been ready to wait four more until her birthday. It was foolhardy and reckless but he'd been dumb with love and he'd thought she was the same way. The way she looked at him, like he'd fixed something that had been wrong in her...she wouldn't look at him like that unless she loved him.

Walter smiled inwardly, remembering this doubt and worry. He wished he could tell himself that he had nothing to worry about. He would barely get the question out before she would say yes.

"Yes," he said and looked at Dale. "This is the one."

"Well," Dale laughed. "No need to rush into this. There are some emeralds here and aquamarines that are very popular."

Walter shook his head. This was Rosie's ring.

"How much?" he asked. "For this one." He held it out to Dale, who carefully took it from Walter's thick and clumsy fingers.

Dale pulled the small sticker from underneath the ring and rolled it into a ball between his thumb and finger.

"One hundred and seventy-five dollars, tax in," Dale said, obviously cutting something off the price.

Walter never knew why Dale did it. Why he lied. Charity or pity or if he really respected the fact that Walter was standing in his jewelry shop with a can of change. Maybe Dale really was that kind. That generous. But at the time, Walter hadn't seen it that way.

"I don't need your charity." The words came out before Walter could stop them.

"It's not charity, son," Dale said, taken aback.

This was the point at which Walter had walked out last time, leaving the beautiful Rosie ring behind. He'd never bought another engagement ring, went so far as to propose at Christmas with nothing to slide onto her lovely hand.

Now, it would be different. He rooted himself to the spot. Dug the fat wad of singles from his front pocket and slid them and the can across the glass counter.

"Thank you, Dale," he said. "I appreciate it."

The past reorganized itself, scenes and moments flipped and flopped, and this ring gleamed from Rosie's ring finger in all of them.

The look on her face when he'd proposed, pulling this dark blue velvet box from the pocket of his coat. The tears and kisses. The way *yes* had tripped from her tongue with surprise and glee, so different from the solemn, serious way she'd said yes before. As if she knew that agreeing to a life with him was going to be work.

She took it off to do dishes every night. Setting it on the windowsill above the sink.

She lost it once, for a week, and Jennifer had found it under the little rug in front of the toilet in the bathroom.

She made him turn back around on the way to the lake one summer, because she'd left it on her bedside table.

"Please," she said, rubbing the naked skin of her ring finger. "I feel so weird without it."

Those last months, she'd lost too much weight to wear it. So he'd strung it on a gold chain and put it around her neck, and every night in the hospital she fell asleep clasping it in her hand.

Jennifer took it in the end. A memento, the gold whisper thin along the band. The pearl as pretty as ever. He didn't know if Jennifer ever wore it. He would like to think that she did, out of fondness for her mother.

And then he remembered the chain and the charm she'd been wearing at his deathbed.

It had been this ring, worn around his daughter's neck and never taken off. A touchstone for her. A piece of the mother she'd loved.

Walter bit his lip against a surprise bark of grief and delight.

Dale Meyers polished the ring and set it in the blue velvet box and Dale didn't even bother to count Walter's money. He had the good grace to act like men came in and bought engagement rings with pennies all the time.

And maybe they did, Walter guessed. Maybe there was something in the act of buying a ring for a woman that reduced men to their bare bones.

Walter walked out of the jewelry store, the ring like a thousand-pound weight in his pocket. His heart like a cloud in front of him and over him. For such a small thing, a ring that in the hot summer months turned Rosie's finger green, the past and the future changed, remarkably.

But he, oddly, was the same.

17

The ride was smooth this time, though the landing was rough and Walter pitched headfirst into the big pine tree in the backyard.

He pulled himself free, only to hear Peter, the shit, laughing at him.

"You're getting the hang of it," he said and Walter scowled, shaking pine needles from his hair.

"Well?" Peter asked, from his vantage point on the swing. He twisted in the swing, wrapping the chains around each other until he could barely touch the ground and then he lifted his feet and spun like a black top.

Beside him, Beth did the same, double dervishes. One ghostly and black, the other diminutive and pink.

"How do you feel?" Peter asked when the spinning stopped. "Redeemed?"

Walter smiled. "I wouldn't go that far."

The little girl walked away from the swing and staggered like a drunk, falling, a giggling mess, onto the muddy ground. Peter watched her with a fond smile, but when he stood, there was no staggering. No feet actually, just that smooth glide toward Walter.

"Great," Peter said. "You've changed your past, gotten rid of some of that sick baggage you carry. So?"

"So what?" Walter asked.

"What day?"

Walter swallowed. Buying the ring hadn't made him ready to lose his wife and daughter all over again. "I thank you, Peter, I really do, for the chance to change that, but I can't go back—"

"Oh, for the love of God," Peter muttered. The earth rumbled, ready to spit out some other filing system that would lead Walter to yet another day of disappointments. "We're just going to have—"

"Peter." Walter stared at the clouds past the top of the pine tree and remembered what the kid had told him at the beginning. That his body was water, mist. The boy was wrong, his leg still throbbed, but he wished it were true. He wished he was wind. Something that floated. Anything but this heavy flesh-and-bone body. "Let me go."

"I can't." The boy shrugged. "Policy—"

"Forget policy!" Walter cried, the volcano of his dormant temper building from his gut. "Forget it." He was a dead man, tired of dying. "Haven't you seen enough?" he shouted up at the sky, blue and white and so bright it hurt his eyes, toward whoever was on the other end of Peter's device. Whoever still pulled the strings. "There's nothing for me to relive. It's all a waste. I missed Jennifer's birth. I didn't get promoted. My wife died and I drank my life away. Buying Rosie that ring doesn't change everything."

"It did for her."

"Well, great! I'm...it did?"

Peter nodded. "What day do you think she relived?"

"The day Jennifer was born." Of course. She was a devoted mother.

"She said..." Peter looked down at the device in his hand and read whatever was printed there "...and I quote, 'Relive thirty hours of labor, alone without Walter? You've got to be kidding me.'"

Walter smiled, imagining her saying that.

"She picked the birthday when you proposed. You changed her life with that ring."

Walter swallowed and took two steps back. Another.

"So, you see, your father. Your wife. You did more good than you think. You were a good man, Walter Zawislak."

"How can you say that?" Frustration bubbled under his skin. "Look at what you've seen."

"I've seen a man trying really hard."

"Look at the days after Rosie died. Look at the days before I met her. Look at the day Jennifer came home from school. I wasn't trying on those days!"

"You're being foolish and shortsighted," Peter chastised him, and Walter felt the weight of his life, the burden of years, on his back.

"And you're being cruel," he whispered, his voice a thin gasp. "This isn't heaven, this is hell."

"Well, it's limbo, actually, we've already talked—"

"I don't care." Walter hitched his pants over a belly he hadn't had when he died. "I am done with this nonsense."

Peter stared at him for a long time and Walter stared back unflinching. If this came down to stubbornness, the boy was in for a world of hurt. Walter had hung on to his life by the sheer force of habit, the stubborn grit of waking up and getting out of bed when he had nothing to live for.

Sunshine faded and wavered behind the eastern trees. Beth's mother stepped out onto the porch carrying a

steaming mug and a sweater for the little girl. She helped
her daughter braid each doll's hair and tie it with pink and
blue ribbons, their earlier fight forgotten.

Peter stood next to them, staring at him with such inten-
sity Walter could feel it. A bird took flight from the tree
behind him. Beth and her mother both turned toward him,
and for a moment it seemed that the three of them on that
porch looked at him with identical blue eyes, gorgeous and
deadly with reproach. Their three faces thin and fierce.

Lights flickered on in houses and the smell of
hamburgers cooking over a fire danced around Walter but
he didn't glance away. Even when the boy's eyes turned
black and gold, and Walter could see in them rivers and
roads and dogs and his house and lawn, trim and tidy and
lush. He saw cannons and war and blood and babies and
the white veil of a bride. He saw everything in those eyes
and Walter was unmoved. He was stone. Granite. A
dead man.

Please, he prayed, unable to speak. *Please let me go.*

"You're not leaving me a choice," Peter finally said.

"That's the idea, kid. Let me go burn in the fire, or whatever is waiting for me, because I am through with your
policy."

Peter blinked, looked away, and mumbled under his
breath about the ungrateful dead and switching jobs. He
started punching things into the device on his hip.

Walter felt the twitchy cool spasms of relief along nerve-
endings.

Good. Fine. Done. Over.

"You're not going to like this," Peter warned.

"I don't like any of it."

This was it. The endless lights out he joked about all the

time. The peace and rest and quiet he'd craved for fifteen years.

His knees went loose and his brain numb.

This is what you want? he asked himself, suddenly wild and frantic with doubt.

Walter reached for the swing set but his ever-shifting body fell through it. He blinked, and the fuzzy pine trees and blurry fence posts reoriented themselves into sharp relief.

His vision was corrected. It had happened. He looked up and saw the glimmering gold edges of the clouds and every blade of grass on the ground.

He laughed. He hadn't been able to see this well without glasses since after the war. It was amazing. "Hey kid—" He turned to see the boy, directly behind him, and realized Peter wasn't so young at all. Lines spidered out around his eyes and creased his thin lips. The boy was a man, really.

And beside him was a men's bathroom door.

"No. No more doors."

"It's policy," Peter said.

Walter, who had never been able to feel the kid when he touched him, found himself being shoved through the door. His forehead smacked the men's bathroom sign and he fell, angry and scared, into an unknown men's room in an unknown part of his life.

18

I t was just a bathroom. White tiled floors, mysterious grunge of a disturbing yellow color in the corner. A man in one of the stalls sounded as if he were in some distress. Walter couldn't place it. It was not a bathroom of major significance as far he could tell.

Not that he had bathrooms of significance.

"What the hell am I doing here?" he shouted. And Peter arrived, looking like Phillip Michael Thomas at the height of the *Miami Vice* pastel craze. Walter guessed this mystery bathroom was in the 80s.

"Patience," Peter said, and Walter thought that if he could, if it was possible, he would strangle Peter with his baby blue suit jacket.

Peter pulled himself up onto the white sink.

"Did you really think you could win a stare down with me? Come on, I've been dead for nine years..."

"Nine?"

"Yep, and you've been dead all of..." he checked his flashy diamond Rolex "...four hours."

"How old were you when you died?" Walter was distracted from his bathroom concerns by the mystery of this ageless young man.

"Why?" Peter swung his sockless, loafered feet.

"I don't know. I just can't seem to get a grip on your age. Sometimes you seem so young, and then I turn around and you look older." Walter leaned against the dark-paneled wall, right by the phone number of Terri, who apparently wanted to have a good time.

"You can be any age you want." Peter laughed. "Everyone just seems to subconsciously choose the age they were the most happy."

Walter looked in the mirror over one of the sinks and realized he was about thirty-two. He palmed the paunch that swelled up over his belt.

He ran a hand through thick brown hair that he had remembered with such passion when all of the gray stuff started clogging the drain in the shower.

Those had been his happiest years, after being married for a few years before Jennifer became such a sullen mystery. He'd just begun to travel for work and Rosie, well... Rosie had been alive.

"So? Which age were you most happy?"

The boy smiled, and before Walter's newly corrected and slow-to-believe eyes, the boy aged. His hair grew white and sparse, and his face creased and folded and sagged along his jowls and under his eyes. Dark brown liver spots bloomed on his forehead and along his crepey neck. His hands became skeletal and his eyes watery. But they still gleamed.

"Any age I want," he said with a toothless grin.

"That is creepy," Walter said, and the boy shook himself

like a dog and his features rearranged themselves back into the fluid young boy Walter recognized.

"I've figured out what's really bothering you," regular Peter said.

"You?"

The boy ignored his joke. "You don't know why they loved you," he said. "You can't figure out why a nice woman would choose you." The truth, like war or death or Rosie leaving him and Jennifer moving on, was unavoidable, a bright light he couldn't run from. "Am I right?" the boy asked, as if he might win a car.

"She didn't think she could have anyone she wanted. She was so insecure. But I knew...I knew she was better than me. She should have had better than me. Better than what I could give her."

"Well..." Peter's smug smile gave Walter chills of foreboding. "I'm going to show you."

There was a knock at the door and they both turned.

"Hello?" a woman's voice called from the other side of the door. "Walter, are you in there?"

That voice wrapped around him like a vice.

"No," he breathed turning on Peter. "Please don't do this. I can't..."

"You didn't leave me a choice."

Peter leaped from the sink and was gone.

The door eased open and a woman poked her head in. Her long brown hair fell over her shoulder. Her eyes were clenched shut.

He was immobile. All the blood and bone and function of his self were gone.

Rosie.

The most beautiful woman he had ever seen. He had

somehow forgotten that after the doctor's appointment and the cancer and the months of wasting.

She glittered and gleamed and sparkled with life. It hurt his eyes; they teared from her brilliance, but he didn't look away. Didn't blink.

"If anyone is in here beside my husband, you better zip up," she warned, then she counted to three and opened her eyes. "Walter?"

"Hi, baby," he whispered.

He shut his eyes and let himself go. Every resistance gone—he floated back to Rosie.

$\sim$

FEBRUARY 21, 1982
Men's Room, Triple R Rolling Rink
Jennifer's 6th Birthday

"WALTER?"

Oh, thank God. Leave it to Rosie to waltz into the men's room to find him. Walter pushed open the door to the john. "Help me," he begged his wife.

Rosie clapped a hand over her mouth. "What have you done?" She dropped her hand but couldn't stop laughing. "Walter..."

"I know, I know," He waddled as best he could out of the tiny stall. "It's supposed to be a surprise."

"Oh!" Her elegant brown brows shot to her forehead. "She'll be surprised. What are you supposed to be?"

He looked down at his green legs and the gray sack that was supposed to be an inflated garbage can around his chest and stomach. The top half of the costume with its suspenders and valves and mask was spread out across the floor like a toilet he might have once taken apart.

"Oscar the Grouch," he muttered. He had ruined it. That much was obvious. "She seems to like him the best." He picked up the fuzzy green arms. "Is she having a good time out there?"

"They're all having a great time," Rosie murmured. He nodded, wondering what to do with the costume. Maybe it wasn't too late to return it, get a full refund.

"Sweetheart?" his wife asked, and Walter looked up at her. The laughter was gone and tears stood out in her brown eyes. "Were you going to roller skate in that?" Her lips curled and Walter laughed.

"Seems dumb, huh?" He started the arduous process of shimmying out of the furry green legs.

"No, no!" Rosie cried, her cool strong hands curling around his wrists. "What are you doing?"

"She's not going to like this, her old man running around in a costume. She's too old—it's a dumb idea."

"Are you kidding?" She stepped close to him, her hands sliding from his wrists to his shoulders to his face. She smiled into his eyes, her own shiny and watery. He could see his reflection in them. He always could. And he never seemed to look as bad as he thought.

"She's going to love it," she whispered. "She's going to love that her dad did this for her. I love that he did this for her."

She stepped closer, making his costume bell out in the rear and he fell backward, awkward and off balance.

She laughed, caught off balance herself, and they collapsed onto the stool. She landed on his lap, her strong, sturdy arms around his neck. Her whispers—*oh you sweet man*—in his ears.

In the end she laced him up. Put some skates on his feet and pushed him out of the bathroom. He was too tall for the costume so he could only see out of half the eye slits, which made skating in a foam garbage can that much more dangerous.

"Oscar!" He whirled to find Jennifer, which made him overstep and correct and nearly fall all within a second.

"Are you the birthday girl?" he asked, hoping the brown pigtails in front of him—all he could see in the dark room— were his daughter's.

She tugged on his garbage can and he crouched down, slipped and landed hard on the knee of his bad leg. He winced and swore under his breath. He would pay for that tomorrow.

"Hello, Jennifer," he said, pulling the costume face down a little so he could see his girl. So pretty in her purple shirt, already looking like so much like Rosie it practically killed him sometimes.

His baby smiled at him, patted the green fur of his costume.

"Hi Daddy," she said.

~

DECEMBER 2, 1980
Jennifer's First Recital
May School Auditorium
Beaverton, Wisconsin

. . .

WALTER STIRRED on the hard wooden seat, struggling to find a comfortable place for his ass on the cracked and peeling auditorium chair.

"Sit still." Rosie glared at him out of the corner of her eye and he shot her an exasperated look.

"If they would start this stuff on time..."

The Clarksons in front of them turned and shushed him, and Rosie glared and Walter stared up at the ceiling, waiting for the night to be over.

She was four, and he loved her, but he could give a shit about the other kids pounding out "Jingle Bells" and "Santa Claus Is Coming to Town." He rolled the program in his hands and hit his knee with it.

"Stop it!" his wife hissed and yanked the program out of his hand. "I should have just left you at home."

The lights dimmed and a spotlight came up on the stage. It roamed for a moment, searching for a target to land on, and finally Mrs. Swenson, the ancient music teacher, fought her way free from behind the red curtain.

She was wearing a Santa hat and orthopedic shoes.

"We will start where we usually do, with the youngest students," she croaked into the microphone without any welcome or small talk. He kind of liked that about Mrs. Swenson. It was just about the only thing he liked about the woman. He had hated her when he was struggling through "Ode to Joy" in the fifth grade with her exhaling the stale stench of coffee and cough drops over his shoulder.

Rosie was convinced they'd been lucky to get Jennifer into private lessons with the old cow and Walter had gone along with it, secretly hating that his daughter would be exposed to Mrs. Swenson's cruel criticism and bad breath.

But Mrs. Swenson had been saying Jennifer showed quite a bit of talent. He and Rosie laughed privately, wondering what a talented four-year-old sounded like playing the piano. They didn't have a piano at home so she practiced at school or before her lessons.

"Though this year our youngest is perhaps our most surprising." With that, Mrs. Swenson lurched and waddled off and the curtains parted. Jennifer sat center stage at the piano. She was a tiny pink confection in frills and ribbons.

Perhaps it was the spotlight or the shining great piano that literally dwarfed his little girl, but Walter fell still and couldn't seem to breathe. He grabbed his wife's hand and could feel her startled and disgruntled gaze at his profile.

She's too little, he thought. *So small to be up there alone. It's too much for a little girl, too much light and too many people watching. This is a mistake.*

Jennifer looked over her shoulder, probably at Mrs. Swenson backstage. Then she turned toward the audience, shielded her eyes from the lights, and looked out at all the parents, most of whom were wishing she would just get on with it.

She seemed to find him and Rosie where they sat left of center in the third row. Rosie waved one finger and Jennifer waved with her whole hand.

"Hi Daddy!" she said. The audience laughed and Walter thought he might black out from lack of oxygen.

"Relax, Walter." Rosie breathed in his ear. "She's going to be fine." Jennifer had to reach up a little to put her fingers on the black and white keys.

"She's too young, Rosie. Look at how little—"

Jennifer bent her head and started to play.

This was what a four-year-old talent sounded like: like wonder. Like blue skies and new grass. Like beauty and cake and Rosie's laugh. Like love and change. Like something completely other than him. Something untouchable and pure and clean.

Rosie's hand gripped his and he knew she was weeping. The Clarksons turned in their seats to stare at them in awed accusation—*You*, their gazes said, *you made this?*

Jennifer leaped and bounced and tiptoed and ran through "What Child Is This?" Everyone in the crowd held their breath, waiting for some stumble, some weird crash back to reality, but it never came. She finished with a small trill. Stood for the stunned and thunderous applause, curtseyed, her black patent shoes blinding in their shine, and ran offstage.

She was four.

"She was perfect," Rosie breathed in his ear. Walter nodded and wondered what he was doing in a family like this.

MAY 12, 1991
    Salesman of the Year Celebration Chili Supper
    The Zawislak Home

WALTER PUT the bottle of champagne under his arm, switched his briefcase to his right hand, and tried to open the door, but the bottle slipped and he dropped the briefcase against the door with a loud clatter to grab the champagne.

The storm door opened and Jennifer stared at him through the screen. "It's just Dad," she called over her shoulder and walked away, giving him the impression that he was just road kill or something equally beneath her notice.

"Hello to you, too," he called after her, kicking his brief-case though the door into the foyer. Rosie said it was a stage, teenage moodiness, nothing but a stage. Walter hoped so. The past year had not been easy; it's not even like he was the bad guy. It's that he was no guy. Nothing. She barely noticed him, his little girl who used to sit on his lap and watch *Sesame Street*.

"Hey babe!" Rosie yelled from the kitchen.

"Hey yourself!"

Tonight, though, nothing was going to get him down. Not his moody daughter. Not the car with the oil leak. Nothing. "Come on out here."

Rosie stepped out from the kitchen, a tea towel over her shoulder and her face red from whatever she was cooking. She pushed up the sleeves of her purple sweatshirt. "What's got into you?" she asked with a laugh.

"You—" he held out his hands and the champagne bottle "—are looking at the Marsden Plumbing Supplies Salesman of the Year."

"What?" she gasped, her brown eyes lighting up. She clapped her hands. "Really?"

"Yep, really." She practically jumped over to him and he snatched her up, pressing the champagne bottle against her side and smacking big, wet, sucking kisses on her neck while she laughed and tried to twist away.

"Oh, sweetheart, that's such great news." She pushed away from him and spun toward the living room. "Jennifer, did you hear the good news?"

"I heard," she cried back over the sound of the Huxtables on TV.

"Well, then come in here and say something to your father..."

"Ros..." he started, hoping to avoid the battles tonight—his night of champagne.

"No, come on," she murmured. "I am so tired of her attitude."

Jennifer stood in the doorway, a thin wisp of a girl in a denim skirt on that painful far edge of childhood. "Way to go, Dad."

"Thanks, Jennifer. Why don't you come sit down at the table with us?"

"Come on, can't we just have dinner in front of the TV?" Her tone of voice was nails on a chalkboard, and Walter wanted to tell her to go to her room, but Rosie squeezed his hand.

"We'll have some champagne," she said.

Jennifer rolled her eyes like she would rather go to the dentist but she took that lazy shuffle forward and he felt Rosie heave a sigh of relief.

"I wish we had something fancier than chili." Rosie ran her hand down Walter's tie and patted his lapel. She looked at him, a saucy sexy look from the corner of her eyes, and his blood warmed.

"It's my favorite."

Rosie pressed her forehead against his chest. "You always say that."

He kissed the top of her head, right where he could see the pink of her scalp. *Thanks*, he wanted to say, *Thanks for convincing your brother to hire me when my own family had given up.*

"It's always true," he said instead. "Whatever you're making is my favorite."

"Are we gonna eat or not?" Jennifer slouched at the table.

"Celebration chili coming right up."

Rosie ran back to the kitchen and brought out the steaming pot and placed it in the middle of the Formica dinette table. She spooned up big bowls and put cheese and sour cream and crackers on them while he pulled the champagne glasses they got for their wedding out of the old hutch in the corner.

He popped the cork and Jennifer jumped and then laughed, embarrassed.

Walter filled one of the delicate crystal bowls with the flowers etched on it and put it front of his daughter.

She sniffed the golden bubbly and turned up her nose.

"You'll like it," he said. "It's sweet."

She took a tentative sip and didn't roll her eyes or make any puking noises so he guessed it was okay.

He handed one to his wife, who sat on the edge of her seat beaming in a sweatshirt splattered with tomato sauce. "To my husband," she said holding the glass aloft. "Salesman of the Year."

Jennifer clapped, which surprised all of them, so he took a bow, making a little production. "Thank you, thank you."

He sat and Rosie grabbed his hand in one of her own and then stretched across the table to grab one of Jennifer's.

He reached out to grab Jennifer's other hand and they both rolled their eyes while Rosie gave thanks over their food.

Faithlessness, or maybe it was just scorn for Rosie's earnest beliefs, was the only thing he and his daughter still had in common.

"Amen," Rosie said, and Walter nodded as had become acceptable after years of Rosie trying to get him to pray.

They dug into their chili, which really was his favorite. The women in his life drank their champagne. And he stared at his, untouched and going flat, out of the corner of his eye. He could taste it—that cloying sweetness on his tongue, the pop and fizz of the bubbles in his nasal cavity—even though he had been fifteen years clean and sober.

He wasn't about to ruin fifteen years, not with a sip, not in celebration.

"Are they gonna throw you a big party?" Jennifer asked.

Walter shook his head. "They took me out to lunch and gave me this..." He pulled an envelope out of his inside jacket pocket and slid it over to Rosie. "We'll be able to fix your car and maybe take a trip to the lake this summer."

Rosie squealed and leaned over the corner of the table to kiss him. "I'm so proud of you," she breathed against his mouth, and Walter felt himself blushing.

She sat back down. "Does this mean you're going to be traveling less?" Rosie asked, and he knew, despite her even tone and her eyes glued to the stem of her glass—all her mustered nonchalance—that she was desperately hoping so.

"I think it probably means the opposite," he said carefully. "My region will probably get bigger and I might be on the road four days a week."

Rosie nodded and took a bite of chili, an arctic freeze blowing off of her. He wasn't happy about it either. Four nights in hotels away from them. But what could he do?

"But I'll be back every weekend," he said. "Al promised."

"Well..." Rosie lifted wet eyes but a determined smile. "If Al promises, it must be true. It will be nice to have you home on weekends, won't it Jennifer?"

"Sure," she said and drained her champagne.

"Whoa!" He and Rosie laughed. "Go easy on that stuff."

Jennifer set down her glass, smiled at the two of them, and then lifted her hand to her mouth and giggled. Her high, girlish giggle made Walter feel like he was being tickled and he laughed, too. And then Rosie started in with her snort laugh and soon they were all coughing and snorting and wiping their eyes with their napkins.

"What's so funny?" Jennifer asked.

And it all started again.

19

No yanking this time. No sickening pull through some terrible loophole in his life and memory. He felt light, like if he lifted his feet he would float. And then he was. Caught on some breeze he was dislocated from the table and the laughter and the smell of Rosie's chili, and he coasted right back into Beth's backyard.

His lush purgatory.

He landed, without the lurch and bounce and crash, on his own two feet. No somersaulting stomach or the belching of bile.

Just the hot run of tears down his face and the shaking that started in his gut and spread out through his life.

It was like no time had passed. He was here. He wasn't and then he was back. Beth finished her last braid and crawled into her mother's lap.

Had it been it seconds? Minutes?

Long enough.

Walter bit his lips until he tasted blood.

He tested those waters, brushed away the dust of those memories, and was flooded. Rosie. Sweet and fine and smiling. Her hair and her breasts, her elegant ankles and her snorting laugh. Her anger and terrible jokes, the dark days after she left. Everything, a wall of Rosie came down on him and he hated it. The pain rippled and shook, and the anger he tried to drink away and forget surged through him. Her beauty, the touch of her hand, the scent of her hair. Those things had faded in his memory and now they were vivid again. Bright and sharp. Real. God, Rosie. His wife. All that love. All the love in the world that he felt for her that he'd spent years trying to purge and dilute with alcohol, it was alive in him. Burning him from the inside.

But with those things, with those gorgeous blessings in his life, came the grief.

And the grief tore him apart.

He'd signed those papers. Broken his promises. Let her go in a cold, cold hospital room. Lost her daughter. Lost himself.

"Walter?"

He was broken. Something deep inside that connected him to his body was fractured and he couldn't get the words out.

I'm scared.

He opened his mouth, but there was nothing but the gasping of air, the lingering duty and work of lungs that hadn't quite realized there was no need for what they could do.

I'm so scared.

He was scared of picking the day. Of seeing Rosie and knowing it was the end.

"Walter? What'd you think? I call it the Jennifer Memory Medley." Peter walked around him to block his view of Beth and her mother. Beth chose that moment to start singing a

Girl Scout song he remembered Rosie singing. The mother laughed and joined in.

"Oh my darling..."

The familiar words curled around Walter's neck, and strangled him. Their sweet high voices slid through the cooling twilight right into the brittle and unused parts of him.

He pressed his clenched fists into his eye sockets.

He was so scared of saying goodbye again.

"Walter, what's wrong? That wasn't so bad. Your wife seems quite nice and your daughter..." He shrugged. "A little bit of an attitude problem, but she was pleasant once you got her drunk."

Beth and her mother messed up the words and Walter flinched when their laughter cut him like shrapnel.

"Oh my daaaaarling Clementine..." They shrieked and giggled and Walter had nowhere to hide. No place left in himself to go to and pretend these things weren't happening.

Rosie and Jennifer used to sing Rosie's old Girl Scout songs at the tops of their lungs. They did it at night. While cleaning. On car trips. He used to beg them to stop. Make a big production of holding his hands over his ears and howling like a dog. It made them sing louder and he had liked that. Appreciated being a part of the joke.

He wondered if, in the silent years between him and his daughter, she ever thought of that.

"You are lost and gone forever, dreadful sorry Clementine!" Beth clapped her hands and her mother jostled her on her knees. Walter took tentative steps toward them as if the ground might collapse under his weight.

He had to stop it. Stop their singing. Their cruel taunting.

"Walter, I really don't understand what your holdup is. There doesn't seem to be much of a contest." The boy lifted his hands. "The way I see it, you've got to pick a day with Rosie, because the rest of your life sucked."

"Light she was and like a fairy..." The mother's voice was cheerful and off-key.

"Walter!" Peter yelled.

"Can't you get them to shut up?"

"What are you talking about?"

"Why are we here with them?" Walter pointed at the women on the porch. "Is this a joke on me? Who the hell are these people?" Walter was screaming, spit flying through the air.

"Walter you need to relax..."

"I don't need to relax. I'm dead." The women sang on, cheerfully rolling through the verses in which Darling Clementine drowns. They were oblivious to his screams and he wanted to tear out his hair. "Just shut them up!"

"You know what you have to do to get out of here and..." Peter took a step between him and the girls, as if to protect them from Walter's ineffective ghostly arms and fists "... leave the girls out of this."

"Out of this? They are a part of my deathbed!" Walter was incredulous and angry. "They are my hell."

"Hell?" Peter gleamed with an unholy light and Walter wondered if maybe he was right. This was hell and Peter was the devil.

"I am telling you this is hell for me."

"You ungrateful man."

"Ungrate—"

"Do you realize the rules I have bent? The never-ending smorgasbord of samples I have given you? The infinite *god damn* patience I have shown? Do you think that's easy?"

Peter stepped close and seemed to grow. And maybe at the beginning of this sickening little trip Walter might have been unnerved or intimidated. But he was unmoved, mired as he was in the rising swamp of his sorrow. "I have every authority to assign you a day—to just pick one, and the way you keep pissing me off, it's not going to be a nice one!"

"Fine. Better that it's a bad day," Walter whispered.

"What is wrong with you? You have a chance to go back and live!"

"Send me to the day Rosie died. The day we put her in the ground. That's the day I deserve."

"Deserve...?" Peter looked lost. "Why? Because you were a soldier doing what soldiers do? Because you signed the papers to get her off the respirator? Because you drank too much?"

"Because I had everything!" Walter yelled. "I had everything and I lost it. I didn't hold on to it. I didn't take care of it. I made promises to people and I never kept a single one. The only thing I ever gave anyone was pain and disappointment. That's why I don't ever want to go back, because there is nothing worse than having it all and ruining it. Leave me here." He threw his arms out to encompass the yard and the women. "Leave me in my hell."

"This isn't your hell," Peter yelled.

"Then what the hell is it?"

"It's my yard you self-absorbed corpse!"

Walter staggered backward, got tangled in his own legs, and sat down hard on the porch.

"Your yard?"

Peter sighed and looked heavenward before collapsing onto a swing. "I am going to get fired. You—" he sent a pointed look at Walter "—are going to get me fired. I should have let Ravi have you."

"What do you mean this is your yard?"

"Well, obviously, *should* be my yard." Peter wrapped his arms around the chains and gazed up at the dark house.

"You said you didn't know these people..."

"I don't. I'm dead."

Walter tried to remember if he had ever seen a father or heard one inside the house. He hadn't.

"Oh no, Peter." Walter stared at the mother who was whispering things Walter could not hear into her daughter's hair. "The little girl...she's your daughter."

"Daughter?" Peter laughed.

"But it's always just the girls and I never see..."

"I think he works a lot," Peter said. "They argue about it. Sometimes at night he comes out here and smokes a cigar."

"So..." Walter was more confused than ever. "Who are these people to you?"

Peter stood up from the swing and floated six inches above the ground staring at the house. "Up in the attic—" he pointed at the small window in the triangular eaves "—way over in the far corner, there's a box with a blue receiving blanket and a wristband from Mt. Sinai and a baseball mitt. There's a couple of other things, some cards and a little silver drinking cup. The box is labeled Peter."

Walter felt an awful stillness, a pain in his chest as realization seeped into his body.

"That's my box. All that they kept of me. All they really had of me." Peter shrugged and turned. "I lived for exactly four minutes and eight seconds. She's not my daughter. She's my sister."

"Peter," Walter swallowed. "I'm sorry."

"You think you're being tortured?" Peter eyes turned hot and red and Walter felt fear. Real fear. "You think it's hard having to pick one day of your miserable gorgeous life to go back to? Try not having the option! Try watching someone deny all that was given them."

"Sam?" The woman called over her shoulder, and Peter and Walter stopped their fight and stared at the girls between them. Beth was asleep in her mother's arms. A tall, slim man who looked exactly like Peter, only older, appeared in the sliding glass door, smiling at his wife.

"Need some help?" he murmured, walking out into the night.

"She's just gotten so big. I can't lift her anymore."

Sam leaned over and slid his arms underneath the sleeping girl, pressing a long, sweet kiss to the woman's mouth while he was down there. He stood, cradling Beth against his chest, her black hair like dark clouds on his sweatshirt.

"Did you hear us singing?" the woman asked.

Sam nodded and headed toward the door. "I taped it."

"Taped it!" She was clearly both horrified and pleased.

"Yeah, through the screen. We can show it to her boyfriends when she's older. It's great."

The woman laughed and patted her husband's butt as they walked through the door into the light of the house. She shut the door behind them.

"You," Peter breathed, looking right into Walter, the grief of a million men on his face, "clearly don't understand torture."

"Why do you do this? Is someone forcing you to watch your family without you?" *Was God so vindictive?*

"Are you kidding?" Peter laughed. "We sign up for this. We line up and fight over these jobs."

"It's so cruel."

"Your limited understanding of that word is laughable," Peter bit out. "They used to give these jobs to people who lived past a hundred. Something about old souls and compassion...go figure. But then someone like you would come along and beg to just be let go, that their life was just too terrible, too full of regret, to be relived. Well, those old souls would just let people slide by, because they understood regret. They knew the pain of having lost something held dear. Well, you can imagine the chaos. So they gave the job to us, stillborns and infants. Because I don't feel compassion for you, do you understand that? I don't feel pity. I'm pissed that you are wasting my time and your life. I never learned to breathe air and I'd give anything—anything—for a day to relive."

Walter wiped his eyes and put his head in his hands.

"Life is beautiful and precious. It's not about mistakes and regret and anger. It's about appreciation and forgiveness. You have forgotten that and you should be ashamed."

Walter shook his head and turned away from Peter and his house with the box in the attic. He understood the sad implications Peter's story had for his own life. But still, he was paralyzed. Lost and scared in the woods, unable to find the tracks that would lead him home.

"I can't," he breathed. "How do I say goodbye again?"

He heard the rumble of the earth that foretold a filing system erupting from some cosmic storage room.

The front door to the Sunrise Café out on Wisconsin Highway 11 emerged from the ground in front of Walter.

"If you're so scared of saying goodbye, let's start with hello," Peter said, just before he kicked Walter in the ass and through the door.

20

As diners went, the Sunrise was top shelf. Sparkling clean, lots of waitstaff and busboys so you never had to wait too long for coffee or tap water. There were plants, real ones, hanging overhead. The booths bordered on plush—ludicrous, almost, with their deep pink padded seats.

Walter had passed out more than once in those booths.

And the spinning pie and cake display was filled with Hulda Allen's homemade peach pies that used to bring people in from as far away as Waterton.

Walter walked over to the peach pie, watched its slow spin on the plastic shelf and had to stop himself from dropping to his knees. He wasn't sure if he wanted to beg Peter to let him go, or thank him for giving him another shot with one of those pies.

"Really, Walter." Peter spun away from the eat-in counter where he sat in a pair of dirty overalls and work boots, like the rest of the men bent over their meatloaf sandwiches. "You have got to be one of the most stubborn files I've ever had."

Walter smiled, watching a coconut cream pie go around. That's what his brother had said about him that day when he thought they were lost. It's what his basketball coach said about him, the guys he served with in the war.

They all said he was stubborn.

Walter wondered if stubborn was supposed to feel so much like scared shitless.

"You know what day this is?" Peter asked, and Walter turned and unerringly found the back corner booth where a young man sat, hat pulled down low over his eyes, pouring whiskey from his flask into his coffee cup. The booth was by the kitchen, in the smoking section even though the young man didn't smoke.

He sat there because it was the new girl's section.

"I know what day it is." He smiled at Peter. Clapped him on the shoulder and walked over to the young man getting drunk on his lunch hour. Walter slid into the booth and sat down in the space the man's earthly body already occupied.

Ask her out, the young man thought. He took a sip of the heavily doctored coffee. *Today's the day; you gotta ask her out.*

Walter smiled, wanted to put his arm around his young self and tell him it was all going to be okay. That today he was going to be a better man than he thought he was capable of being. But instead he swallowed and pushed into the center of his young self. Into his brain and bone and skin, into his worry and constant despair, into his fear and his fragile secret feelings for the new girl.

MAY 28TH, 1973
    Sunrise Diner
    Back Corner Booth

.   .   .

"HERE YOU GO." The new girl slid a giant piece of pie across the table in front of him.

He smiled though he couldn't quite look at her. Like the reflection of the sun off the corner of a windshield, she was something he watched out of the corner of his eye.

"Thanks, that's some piece of pie." He swiped a finger under a fat slice of peach that was crowded off the plate. "Hope you left some for the next guy."

"Well, I don't think there will be too many next guys. The lunch crowd is pretty much gone."

Walter looked up and realized the restaurant was practically empty. He should get going. Christopher had given him shit yesterday for coming back late from lunch and he knew that it was only a matter of time before Christopher told him to stop coming to the site.

"Mind if I...?" the new girl asked and Walter, surprised, finally took his first good look at her. Brown hair, brown eyes. She was round. Round cheeks, round shoulders. Round lovely breasts pushing at the front of her pink and green striped uniform—all things he had the impression of from his surreptitious watching, but were lovelier than he had imagined while filling in the blanks.

"Do you mind if I join you?" she asked again. She tilted her head and smiled, and Walter's heart stopped dead in his chest.

I'm a goner.

"Yeah, yeah, of course. Sure." He gestured at the big soft pink bench across from his. She gratefully sat down and scooted across until her side was pressed to the wall.

"It's nice to sit down," she breathed. "I'm working a double today and it's not going to be pretty."

He laughed and didn't know what to do with his hands, so he balled them up in his lap.

"What's your name?" She flipped over the unused mug on her side of the table, poured herself a cup of coffee from the pot she had with her, and then set the nearly empty pot on the table. She cradled the cup in both hands like she was cold, and Walter wished he had a jacket to offer her or something.

"I'm Walt...Walter."

"Hi, Walt Walter. I'm Rosie."

"It's just..." he started, but she smiled and he realized that he was being teased. Him. Teased. He didn't quite know what to do with himself.

"Nice to meet you." She held out her hand and he braced himself for the touch of her skin, that lovely smooth slide of her palm into his. He braced for it and it still zapped him down to his feet.

"Nice to meet you, too," he said. Her handshake was really strong for a woman, her fingertips soft.

"You gonna eat that pie?" She nodded toward the slice of pie that was collapsing under its own weight.

"Yeah, of course." He grabbed his fork and shoveled a sugary, sunny slice of peach into his mouth. He pointed his fork at the plate. "God, that's good pie."

Rosie laughed, "I'll take your word for it."

Walter sat back, feigning great shock. "You've never had one of Hulda Allen's peach pies?"

"No." She smoothed an awkward hand down the front of her uniform. "But I am glad you like it."

"You want a bite?" He inched the plate toward her.

"No, no. Thanks, but no."

His fork hit the plate and it was loud and he was blushing. He was no good at this. A terrible flirt, no sense of what was right or wrong. He coughed and kept eating the pie, though now with a painful sort of awareness. Surely he was going to drop the whole thing in his lap or some other ridiculous thing.

"You've been sitting in my section for weeks now and I haven't seen you smoke one cigarette."

It was sort of like an accusation. "I don't smoke," he said and took a sip of coffee/whiskey, wishing he were better at this.

"So why do you sit here?" She rested her head against the wall and smiled at him like they were old friends already. Like she already knew all of the bad stuff about him and was still willing to sit there and smile.

He put down the coffee mug.

"Because the new girl brings me huge pieces of pie." He smiled back at her, but quickly turned his focus to the grey day outside the window when he started to feel too bold.

"My, my." Rosie smiled. "I do believe you are flirting with me."

"Uh...not...really." He went for another drink, anything to give him something to do rather than look into those eyes and wonder if she was laughing at him.

But his coffee cup was empty. Rosie lifted the pot and poured the last of the coffee into his mug.

"Thanks," he muttered, his hand fumbling in his pants pocket for his flask.

"I like that you're flirting with me," she said. "I've been waiting for you to talk to me for weeks now."

"Really?" His voice sounded like a thirteen-year-old boy's, and he cringed and coughed.

"Yeah, here or..." She shrugged. "I know your family goes to my church and I keep hoping that one of these Sundays you might show up."

"That's nice... I mean... that you—" He wished he could

swallow his tongue. "I don't spend much time at church." He unscrewed the lid of his flask and slid his coffee cup toward the edge of the table.

"Please don't do that," she whispered and Walter stilled.

"Do what?"

She nodded her head at his hand, which gripped the flask under the table. "I want to get to know you and I think you want to get to know me. I mean, I can't figure out why else a guy would sit in the smoking section day after day when he's not a smoker." She smiled, but it seemed sad to Walter. She put her hand on his where it gripped the mug, and his whole body twitched.

His heart made some arcane calculations. Subtraction and minuses of sums that were less than or greater than others. Fractions and equations figured in the chemistry and blood of his gut and the sudden electrical currents he felt, gazing upon her face.

Walter screwed the cap back on his flask, not at all sure what was happening.

He put both hands back on the table, suddenly feeling taskless and unmoored. A drinker without a drink.

"What do you do for a living, Walt Walter?" she asked, her smile bright again, and he was pleased in some deep place that he could do that. That he had the ability to make her smile glad.

"I'm working on the plumbing out at the new school." He jerked his thumb behind him toward the Highway 10 cutoff.

"Oh, I bet you know my brother, Al. He owns Marsden Plumbing Supply."

"Al's your brother?" Walter asked. He really liked Al, a straight shooter with a big laugh, a salesman who never seemed to be selling anything. He didn't deal directly with Al, as foreman, Christopher did, but he always took a few minutes to shoot the shit with the big guy when he came by. "I guess I can see the family resemblance." He ducked his head so he could see into her face. "It's your eyes."

"You mean it's the family shape you recognize." Rosie blushed again and he loved it. Just adored that color on her cheeks. "Round. Al and I are both round."

"Well…" Walter laughed. "If Al is your brother, then yes, I'd say he's round, but you are…" He realized too late where his stupid mouth was taking him. He stopped abruptly and the blush on Rosie's face turned blotchy at the neck, and her smile was determined rather than glad or bright.

"Round—"

"Perfect," Walter interrupted pushing the word out before he went cowardly. "Very, very—" He cleared his throat and concentrated hard on making sure his coffee cup lined up right with his napkin. "Perfect."

Rosie pressed her finger down on a grain of salt that was on the table and swept it away. "Thanks," she breathed.

"You're welcome," Walter said, wishing he could have a drink. He took another bite of the pie, despite the fact that he was so full he was about to bust.

"I think maybe I would like a bite of pie." Walter, his mouth full, nodded, probably with more enthusiasm than a bite of pie warranted, and pushed the plate toward her. She picked up a fork and grinned at him, looking like nothing so much as a little girl about to do something wicked.

"Better be as good as you say it is."

"Trust me."

She speared a slice of peach sitting in a small pool of juice and cinnamon along with a little of the flaky crust, and with great delicacy, which fascinated Walter to no end, she put the bite in her mouth.

She closed her eyes and moaned. "Oh, that's good."

Walter's blood warmed, watching her eat the pie.

She laughed, a girlish silly sound, and speared another bite. Walter was suddenly starved for peach pie and the two of them finished off the slice.

"Oh my lord, it will be nothing but water and grapefruit for days..." Rosie sat back and put her hands over her belly. He loved the way she ate, the way she really seemed to relish it. He liked peach pie, but he never closed his eyes and moaned over it.

He brushed some crumbs off the table while the blood beat in his erection.

"What...what happened to your neck?" Her fingers fluttered over her own carotid artery.

That took care of the erection in a big hurry.

Walter tilted his head to try and stop the sudden burning of his scar.

"Were you in the war?" she asked.

Walter nodded.

"So was Al."

"Really?"

"Yeah, he doesn't talk about it much...he came home a few years ago and just threw himself into work. Worked like he was on fire." She took a sip of coffee. "Are you like that?"

"Like what?" Walter asked, still trying to put it together in his head that the big laughing Al was a vet like him.

"Working like you're on fire?"

He shook his head. "Can't say as I am. Working like I'm fast asleep, maybe."

"Was that—" She gestured, something between a point

and a wave, at his neck and Walter had to fight to keep himself on the bench. If Al was a vet, didn't she know she shouldn't point? Shouldn't draw attention to the ruined generation coming back from that place? His hand fell to his pocket and the flask and the salvation.

"I'm sorry," she muttered. "I shouldn't ask. I just...I wish Al would talk. You know, just...talk to me. I just want someone to talk to me about it."

She was waiting for him to answer or respond like a normal person in a normal conversation would, but he wasn't normal. The silence stretched and stretched until he felt compelled to say something or throw the empty coffeepot at the wall.

"If he wants to talk, he'll talk." Walter shrugged. "I guess."

Rosie leaned forward. Her hands were in her lap and he could see where the table cut off her arms. The skin was white and when she leaned back there would be angry red lines across all that pretty skin. He wanted to ease her back so she wouldn't do that to herself.

"Do you want to talk?"

"About the war?" he asked, horrified.

She bit her lip and nodded. "About anything."

He didn't know how to answer these questions. He wanted her to stop biting her lip. He wanted to kiss her and hold her, press his nose to her neck. But he had nothing to say. Nothing at all. He was such an empty thing inside. There were just echoes and memories and whiskey.

She sat back and there were the red marks on her arms and he wanted to touch them with his thumbs. With his lips.

"I'm not much of a talker," he finally told her.

She watched him for a long time, waiting maybe for him

to change his answer. Walter started to get the feeling that there was something else at work here. Something underneath the pie and the talk and her beautiful flesh.

There was a choice buried in all of this.

She nodded and started scooting away from the wall toward the aisle. "I better get back to work before my boss starts yelling." She grabbed the empty coffeepot on her way. "Well, thanks for sharing the pie..."

She stood up and he realized what was happening, how the empty spots were getting bigger and that this was the first time in a long time he wasn't angry or drunk. He realized that this woman was gold and that if she walked away —this choice was made.

She stood and he stood, as well. "I'm not much of a talker," he told her again. "But then, I've never had anyone real keen to listen to whatever I might say..."

"I would listen," she said without a smile or grin or girlish laugh, and Walter could see all the worth of this woman, the things down deep that she would keep hidden from people. The pain and the regret and the worry and the wishes. He could see all of it.

I am going to marry her, he thought and decided he'd better get worthy of Rosie in a hurry.

"I..." He took a deep breath. "I would like to take you to dinner some time. A movie? Or something? Is that...would that be..." He was stammering and stuttering and being an idiot. He looked back out the window, like the gray day might have something to add to this terrible attempt at courtship.

"I would like that," she finally breathed, and Walter thought that maybe the gray day wasn't so gray anymore.

"Friday?" he asked.

"Today is Friday," she said.

"Oh, right. Next Friday?"

"Tonight's fine. My double is over at six."

He nodded and found himself smiling like a fool. Just nodding and smiling, standing in a restaurant asking the new girl out on a date.

"All right, tonight then."

"It's a date." She hugged the coffeepot to her chest like it might leap away from her.

"I guess so."

In a bold move that Walter would learn through the years was really quite out of character, Rosie leaned in to him and was about to press her soft pink lips to his cheek, where the scar licked up from his neck. The first of a million such blessings and benedictions that would pull Walter back to life.

But just before her lips touched his flesh Walter was swept away from the Sunrise Café out on Highway 10. He was pulled away from Rosie and his salvation and dropped back into Peter's backyard.

"Hey!" Walter whirled trying to find Peter in the dark yard. "We weren't finished. She was going to kiss me." He couldn't find the boy in the shadows. It was night. The middle of the night by the depth and texture of the quiet that filled the little backyard like wool. Walter looked up at the full moon that filled the eastern sky.

Suddenly there was nothing Walter wanted more than to feel his wife's lips against his again. It had been twenty years and the thought now consumed him.

"Peter!"

One more kiss.

The wedding kiss? He could relive that day, but it had

been a fairly chaste little number. And that night Rosie had passed out so there was no wedding night bliss to relive.

Their first kiss. Which, if he remembered, was on their third date. Or was it second? He wasn't sure, but the kiss stood out. Though messy, it had led to some pretty heated necking in the back row of that movie theater.

He wanted to touch her. Feel her again. Look into her eyes and see his reflection there. He wanted to hear a bad joke...he wanted it all.

He wanted his wife back, with the same ferocity that had led him back to the bottle after the doctor's appointment changed their lives.

"You have to say goodbye to her, Walter."

"What? No—I did that already."

"I understand it's hard. You were soul mates."

"Please." Walter scoffed at the notion, but inside, in his heart and his gut and his soul, he wept in agreement. *We were. She was.*

"Walter, you didn't kill her. The cancer—"

"I signed the papers. I said okay. I didn't stop the doctor that came in and turned off those machines. I stood there and let it all happen. My—" He stopped, realizing he was crying. Spitting. Oh, this grief. This anger. When would it go away? "She wanted to die at home and I promised I would do that. I promised I'd take care of our daughter. That I wouldn't drink. I broke all of them, every single one."

"Come on." The boy sighed heavily through his nose. "Let's deal with this."

"What?"

There was no warning. No door. No tap-tapping on Peter's stupid fucking phone. One minute he was in the backyard, the next he was standing in hospital hallway a few feet away from himself, young but aging by the second. Grief was making a scarecrow out of him. Jennifer, young and desperate, stood in front of the scarecrow.

"Please, Dad," Jennifer was begging. "Please Dad, don't take her home. Don't—"

"She wants to die in her bed, honey." He was breathing, trying to be reasonable, sympathetic even, when all he wanted was to drink the entire situation away. He remembered that clearly. How weak he'd felt in the face of Rosie's sickness, how it called to the worst of him. "I promised—"

"But it was so fast. They still haven't tried everything. The doctor said there was a chance she might respond—"

"She's dying, sweetheart." The younger him reached out to touch her shoulder but Jennifer slapped his hand away.

"One week." Her eyes blazed, and he'd been scared of the anger and hate in her eyes, scared because he felt it, too. "One more week."

"Okay," he promised, and he and Jennifer walked down the hallway, side by side but with a gaping crevice between them that would only get worse.

"You broke that promise for your daughter," Peter whispered and Walter nodded, watching himself and his daughter walk away.

"It was for me, too. I wasn't in any hurry to care for her at home. I didn't know how to say goodbye to her like that. How to do the things that needed to be done for her."

"That's only human," Peter said.

"But I was the adult," he said. "I should have...I should have acted like it."

"Well, you did, didn't you?" Peter asked. "Eventually."

Speechless, Walter nodded.

One week later his beautiful wife had been on life support and he'd acted like the adult and ended it all.

The hallway spun, the wall behind them flipped, and they were suddenly in the hospital room.

He stood beside himself at Rosie's deathbed.

"No!" He bolted, ran for the door, but the boy got in his way, and for being a damn ghost he was suddenly very solid, and Walter in his rage and grief couldn't get past him. "Don't," he begged. "Please don't do this to me."

"You're doing it to yourself, Walter. It's okay. What you did, what you had to do. It was the right thing. Look at it, now. With new eyes. Please. For your own sake."

The right thing. That's what he'd told himself through the grief, through Jennifer's hate. But somehow, over the years, drowning in a sea of booze, the person who'd signed those papers became someone he hated, an entity outside of himself. Or maybe of himself—those pieces he so rarely used after her death—his reason and cold rationality, his practicality and pragmatism. Over the years the hate and grief and blame he had nowhere to put got heaped on those parts of himself he longed to deny. Much like his part in Rosie's death.

Yes, it had been the right thing, but that didn't mean he hated himself any less for doing it. For getting it all wrong.

"She won't feel any pain?" he heard his living self ask, and slowly he turned, coming face to face with himself in this horrifying panorama.

There were the nurses, so busy with all the little tasks that accompanied killing someone. The removal of IVs, the last administering of pain meds. All these women, who for weeks had called him by name, brought him coffee from the nurses' station, asked after Jennifer while caring for his dying shell of a wife—now they wouldn't even look him in the eye.

Probably because of the way he'd dealt with Jennifer,

asking her to leave if she was only going to scream at him. Shameful. If Rosie had been able she would have torn a strip off him.

But now, when he needed someone by his side, someone to pat his hand and tell him he was doing the right thing, now the nurses were too busy to make eye contact.

"No pain," said the doctor with stone-faced sympathy. His cool medical reasons for taking Rosie off life support had finally convinced Walter to sign the papers, largely because he'd been unable to stand it anymore. Sitting by her bed day in and day out, watching machines force her to breathe, had worn him down to nothing—to frayed nerve endings. And Jennifer, Jennifer's hope had been so damn tragic. She'd never seemed to understand that Rosie wasn't going to get out of that bed. Ever.

And when he'd told Jennifer his plans...well, it hadn't gone well.

Look at her, he thought, staring down at his wife. The tubes and the machines, the IVs and the monitors. None of which she'd wanted, she'd made that clear after her diagnosis. She'd wanted to die in bed, in her home.

"I'm sorry," he whispered to Rosie, making his way between the living version of himself and one of the nurses. She was there, his wife, his soul mate, under the pale skin, the red scabs, and chafe. Her hair was gone and she'd lost too much weight, but his Rosie was there. Beautiful and sweet and dying.

With or without his help.

"I should have listened to you," he whispered, touching her hand, her face. He could feel her heartbeat, her warmth, and tears burned in his head. Thousands of them, unshed for so long. "I should have opened the bedroom window so you could smell the lilacs. I should have held your hand and dressed you in your favorite nightgown. I should have—" He choked, curling over her, pulling her body into his ghostly arms. "I should never have let it come to this. And I'm sorry I didn't keep the rest of my promises. I'm sorry I started drinking, and Jennifer —" He couldn't continue, not without making a mess of himself.

"Okay," the living version of himself said, his voice as fractured as he remembered feeling inside, a thousand pieces never to be put back together.

Walter closed his eyes and listened to the tapping of machines, the slowing of beeps. *Dying*, he thought, hiding his face in her neck, smelling her despite the hospital. Despite his dying senses.

Behind him there was a strangled gasp and he turned to face himself. Eyes full of tears, the beginning of a self-hate so powerful it would ruin the rest of his life, the living Walter stood rock still. His nostrils flared as he tried desperately to suck in enough air. Walter remembered all of it, the sensation of drowning, his inability to reach for her hand because he was frozen. Frozen in panic.

Was he doing this? he'd wondered. Was he really killing her like this?

Oh god, that poor man, Walter thought and he backed away from his wife, his instincts gone haywire. And slowly, carefully, unsure of the rules or what would happen if he crossed this particular dead/living line, he wrapped his arms around the grieving man in front of him.

"It's okay," he whispered, soaking in his own words, letting them right certain wrongs in his gut, his heart. "You did the right thing."

Listening to the beeps get farther and farther apart, until there was nothing but deafening, crushing silence. Waiting for the doctor's too-loud voice to say "Time of death, 8:38 a.m," he held onto himself and he didn't let go.

Not for a long time.

He thought of the river, the war. The bubble of champagne in a glass. The love that saved him.

"You did the best you could," he whispered.

21

Walter floated up out of the hospital, through concrete and steel beams, up into the sky, past birds and clouds, right back into Peter's back-yard. And the floating was like those dreams he'd had when he was kid. The flying dreams, the ones he woke up from convinced that something magical had happened in the night and he was now unaffected by gravity.

The sky was starless, a thin cloud hovered over the moon, and Walter wished he could see the Milky Way. It had been a long time since he'd seen that, too many years since he took the time to notice a pretty, clear night. Slowly, while he watched, the great trail of glitter and stardust appeared across the curve of the night sky.

Walter soon remembered that he had never seen the Northern Lights, and while he had never given them much thought while he was alive, he realized right now, four hours and however minutes dead, he wished he had seen them.

And suddenly, low in the northern sky, there they were. The dancing brilliant green, red, and blue phantasms.

"Well, I guess you figured it out. You're really dead." Peter said. "You still hungry?"

Walter shook his head. His body was light, fluid almost. He couldn't quite tell the difference between his flesh and the night air.

He wondered if Rosie had felt this. If, when he had signed those papers and the plug had been pulled and the beeps of the heart rate monitor and the gasp and clang of the oxygen finally slowed and then stopped in terrible silence, if the pain and earthly disease dissolved and she became weightless.

He hoped so. He wished he could see it. He smiled at the thought of Rosie floating, taking huge spaceman leaps into the air.

At once Walter realized what this relived day might be. The very last time he would ever see his wife.

Walter was used to fear; he had been scared his whole life of one thing or another. But he realized all of the long tangled ends to those fears were tied to into one knot. Walter was scared that in those endless, countless arguments with Rosie about heaven, that he had been right.

That there was no heaven. Not for men like him.

"What happens...after?" Walter whispered. He looked at Peter with eyes that were clear and focused in a way he wasn't sure they had ever been.

"After?"

"After I relive a day?"

"Ohhh." Peter nodded and pursed his lips. "The heaven or hell question."

"Yeah." Walter cleared his throat. "I mean, for me, what is it?"

"Well, hell is actually quite a bit harder to get into than you humans seem to think. It takes lots more than sex before marriage and eating pork to land you in the fiery pits."

"But the war...? Those men—"

Peter shook his head. "You've paid enough for those things."

Walter blinked rapidly up at the sky, but his worries were not put to bed. In life, after the war, he'd no longer *believed*. Surely there had to be punishment for that.

"To get into hell, it has to be crimes against humanity sort of stuff. The vicious and evil and the—"

"Faithless?" Walter asked.

"Nope. Even the blind, dumb, and stupid ones get a chance at heaven." Peter smiled and then frowned. "I called you blind and stupid, and you've got nothing?"

"So," Walter breathed, looking deep inside for those tracks in the snow. "What's heaven?"

"It's what you've always thought it was."

"But what if I thought it was nothing? That it didn't exist?"

"Heaven is what you want." Peter shrugged. "If that's what you wanted..."

Walter barely heard him over the echo of Rosie in his ears, saying that his years of faithlessness weren't going to get him any favors when he died. She'd always laughed and said she was going to be waiting for him on a cloud somewhere dressed in her prettiest wings, and he was going to be a no-show unless he started working on believing in something. Anything.

He had joked and wisecracked and remained...what had the kid called him? Stupid, and blind.

So blind, and this was his payment.

"What if I made a mistake? What if I was wrong believing what I did?"

"I think it's been proven a few mistakes have been made in your life. But I told you at the beginning there are no do-overs."

Walter scrubbed at his eyes, rubbing away the tears, and turned back to the sky, conjuring up falling stars so he wouldn't fall onto the earth and sob.

He watched the Northern Lights and wished that he and Rosie had been able to take Jennifer north, maybe to Minnesota.

"We never went camping," he said aloud. "We should have done that. Camped."

"Don't do this to yourself, Walter. Don't count your regrets."

"Do you have any idea how much television I watched? I mean, it was bad enough at home, but on the road. All those nights of room service and bad television. Those big beds and nice sheets, wasted on me and reruns of *Hill Street Blues*." He shook his head. "Obviously, the room service was a bad idea. Rosie was a good cook, healthy stuff that didn't taste bad, but traveling as much as I was..." He patted his chest. He shook with nerves and adrenaline. "Too many cheeseburgers."

"Walter..."

"I should have made Rosie feel better about herself. More compliments. I should have listened and tried—" He linked his fingers together to stop the shaking.

"Walter!"

"I didn't want to see her again, you know? I didn't want to say goodbye all over again. And now all I want is to see her and it will be the last time, won't it? This is it for Rosie and me. I pick a day, I go back and kiss her and hold her, and then...no more."

Walter turned and a young boy stood there. A young Peter, about five years old.

"You're out of time," the boy said in Peter's serious way.

Those wasted years stood around him like sentinels, markers of those times he'd run aground in his grief and faithlessness. It was laughable, those things he'd been afraid of then—love and hurt and being alone—compared to what he was now facing.

The end. His last chance at life, at touching what had been so good and then so forgotten.

Suddenly in the thick, moist grass that gleamed with velvet texture in the moonlight Walter saw the footprints that would lead him back home, out of the wilderness.

"June 16, 1991."

"Pardon?"

"That's the day. That's the day I want." Walter stood. "June 16, 1991."

"You're sure?"

"I'm sure."

"No fooling around anymore Walter. I've got people backed up. Wandering down that hallway freaking out—"

"I'm sure! I'm sure. Let's just get this over with."

A podium erupted from the earth, and Peter twitched and was once again full-grown.

"That's an interesting trick," Walter said.

"You can do it, too," Peter told him and opened a very small and thin laptop. But Walter wasn't interested in tricks.

Peter tapped a few keys and shook his head. "That day is not on your list."

"Does that matter?" Walter asked, suddenly panicked that in the end this would be taken away from him. "You said any day."

"Sure, right, fine. Any day. It just doesn't seem to be an important one."

Walter smiled. "It's important."

"All right, then. June 16, 1991, it is." The contract appeared, and Peter held the paper and a pen out to Walter.

Walter signed the contract with a shaking hand, but when Peter grabbed it Walter refused to let go. "Wait! Wait. Let me just be sure. I get the whole day and when it's over it's over. It's the last time I see Rosie."

Peter smiled and then laughed. "I told you, Walter." Peter leaned in close and Walter could feel his breath against his scar. "You've got to have a little faith."

22

June 16 1991

Walter drifted toward wakefulness, growing aware that his wife's cold hands had eased into his boxer shorts. He sighed, enjoying Rosie's amorous intentions.

"You awake?" she whispered in his ear, her body pressed up close to his back.

"I am now." He breathed deep of the lilac breeze that floated in through the screen. Rosie had insisted on planting that damn bush by their bedroom window. It was nice at times like this, but it attracted every insect known to man at the end of May and beginning of June.

He rolled over to face her, keeping his eyes shut so that the first thing he saw would be her. It was ridiculous; he knew it, was nearly embarrassed by it as if someone might know he was behaving like some teenager.

But that was what love did to Walter.

He had been gone for a week on business, and missing his wife was like having a rock in his shoe. He couldn't do anything without thinking about her.

And being back home over the weekends, these days made him feel almost tipsy. Mellow and convivial.

He opened his eyes and there she was. A red crease across her forehead from the pillowcase and that warm, warm look on her face that always went straight to his groin.

The morning light came in through the window and hit her brown eyes in such a way that they looked like fine brandy.

They were as potent as all the cheap brandy he had guzzled over the years.

She smiled and leaned in close. "Good morning," she whispered deliberately blowing her foul morning breath over his face.

He did not understand this little joke. This little routine of theirs that for whatever reason she found so funny, but he played along because her hand was doing fantastic things in his shorts.

"You been eating shit in your sleep again?" He said his line and she laughed.

"You're hilarious," she said and began pressing kisses to his neck, across his scar that he knew long ago she stopped seeing. His scar, she had told him once, was like his eyes or his broken nose, it was just part of what made up the looks of the man she loved.

He touched her back through the blue silk of her slip and kissed her shoulder where the blond lace had slid down her arm.

"I'm the luckiest man alive," he told his wife.

"No foolin'," she told him.

Rosie glared at him in the mirror as she clipped on her right earring.

"You promised," she said and started to button her bright blue shirt and tuck it into her matching skirt. "Last week, you promised. And so did Jennifer."

Walter stretched and kicked at the sheet that covered his legs. They were nice sheets, like the ones in the fancier hotels he stayed in on business trips. He had asked Rosie to buy the expensive sheets and she'd complained at first about the money, but now they couldn't sleep on anything else. Their bed was a Taj Mahal for a good night's rest. And frankly, right now, he wouldn't mind a little more time in bed. An extra hour of sleep.

"But Rosie, the lawn, and the car needs an oil change and—"

"I don't care." She turned, her hands on her hips. "You promised you would go to church this week. Seriously Walter, I am not asking you to join the priesthood. I ask for one Sunday a month."

"I know, but the—"

"If you say the lawn I swear to god I will go out there and pull the whole thing up."

He smiled, but when the heat ratcheted up in her eyes he quickly squelched it. Apparently Rosie was serious about this. "Okay. We will go to church."

"Good." Rosie leaned over him and pecked his lips. "I knew you would see it my way."

That was the magic of their relationship—she could always get him to see things her way.

She swiveled back to the mirror and gave herself one last look. And apparently wasn't happy. "What do you think?" she asked, smoothing her hands down her hips. "I look pretty wide, don't I?"

He didn't know how to answer these questions. He always told her the truth, that she was perfect, gorgeous, but it never seemed to do much for the way she saw herself. He didn't understand it.

"Baby." He threw the sheets off his legs and stood. "I told you, you're perfect." He stroked her long brown hair and kissed her forehead. "Beautiful."

He walked past her to the bathroom, wishing he could just put on his shorts and go mow his lawn rather than fight with their daughter, watch his wife fight with their daughter, and sit through one of Father Kennedy's sermons.

There were a million things he'd rather do.

WALTER LOCKED the door behind him and followed Rosie and Jennifer toward the garage. His daughter was all in black and he had wanted to tell her to change, that she looked like she was going to a funeral rather than to church, but Rosie stopped him.

She gave him her old pick-your-battles argument and Walter listened, but the whole time he was thinking what Jennifer really needed was a good swat across the butt. If she was going to behave like a two-year-old then she should be...

He cut off his thoughts, feeling the hard beat of blood in his neck that signified an increase in blood pressure.

Doctor said he needed to relax more.

"You coming?" Rosie asked over her shoulder and Walter nodded.

The sun was shining, the hum of a lawnmower and the smell of fresh-cut grass wafted over the fence from the Pillens' house next door.

He bounced his keys in his hand, enjoying the sun on his head and the lax bonelessness from having made love.

Maybe he could convince them both to go get root beer floats after church. It seemed like that kind of day.

"When are we going to get an automatic garage door?" Jennifer asked. She and Rosie stepped out of the way as he heaved the old door up.

"When you win the lottery."

Jennifer rolled her eyes.

In the cluttered gloomy darkness of the garage sat the old beige Parisienne.

"When are we going to sell this old car?" Rosie asked. He stroked his wife's hair, which she had left loose after he asked her to, and languished in the soft vanilla scent of her lotion.

"Never," he answered, kissing her ear. "I want to be buried in this car."

He loved this car, this terrible relic from the gas guzzling seventies. The Millennium Couch as Jennifer called it, and it was like driving a recliner down the road.

"Can we put a limit on the PDA? We're going to church." Jennifer scowled like she was the authority on appropriate church-going behavior. She slammed the door shut behind her before lying down flat in the back seat.

"Yeah," he said to his wife before squeezing her hips. "Enough with the PDA."

She swatted his hands away and they both wedged their way past the junk and clutter he never seemed to find time to throw away.

"You have got to do something with all this crap." Rosie ducked past the wood from the oak he had pulled down last year. He was going to build a chest for her as soon as he found the time.

"After church, I promise."

"Walter?" He looked up to meet his wife's eyes across the top of the car. "I really appreciate this. Church and everything."

He smiled and slid into the plush seat of his car.

The engine started with a jump and roar, and he hit all four of the automatic window switches making the glass descend halfway into the door with a hum and whir.

Rosie, seeming to understand his mood, turned on the radio and switched it from AM to FM and found their favorite oldies station.

She tapped her fingers along to the Supremes and he put the car into Reverse.

"Let's take the long way," Rosie suggested.

"Come on..." Jennifer whined.

"Sounds good," Walter agreed and backed up out of the dark garage into the bright morning.

CHURCH WAS CHURCH. He wouldn't have minded going if it weren't for all the religion. He nodded at friends. Shared a few jokes with some of the guys from the VFW who got dragged here with their wives. He liked this part, the chitchat and sitting in a room full of people he knew. Didn't care much for the singing.

Jennifer fell asleep and he had to jostle her with his elbow. He stood. He held his half of the hymnal. He tried very hard to focus on what Father Kennedy was saying, tried to repent for the years of neglect toward his soul. But he couldn't concentrate on any of it.

The light was shining through the stained glass windows behind the altar. He had no clue what was being depicted in those windows, but it was blood and gore from the looks of things, and he was not inclined think about anything unpleasant, anything war-ish.

It was beautiful, this sunshine. As beautiful as the goodness of people in his community. He didn't understand why they needed to come here to know that. Why did everyone need to believe in something other than themselves and their families? Rosie always said that church made her feel less alone, that she was loved despite all her earthly flaws, and he always said that *she* made him feel less alone and more worthy of love.

Some cloud outside must have shifted away from the sun because the light turned up a notch and in the windows the ruby red of the blood, the blue of cloaks, the emerald of trees, and the bright white of beards were illuminated and the colors fell in blocks across the carpet and onto the uplifted faces of the folks in the pews. There were red spots in the white hair of the Maries in front of him, green splashes across Mike Rogers' face, and Sarah Pillen's mouth and neck were checkered blue and yellow.

Walter was suddenly taken with the notion that those people were being anointed. Marked for a later higher purpose, their goodness noted and sanctified. He turned and looked at Rosie, her brown hair lit with red and his daughter blinking and trying to dodge the yellow beam that was falling across her eyes.

He looked down at his lap, expecting nothing. His hands, resting on his knees, were bathed in bright purple light.

Walter turned his hands over and cupped the light in his palms.

"I'M GONNA PRACTICE." Jennifer shrugged off her jacket and threw it at the coat rack by the door. It landed in a lump on the floor, but his daughter was already on her way to her room. They got her a piano a few years ago. A cheap used thing she made sound like it cost a million bucks.

Walter tossed the keys onto the little telephone table Rosie bought a few weeks ago, and Rosie picked up Jennifer's jacket and hung it up properly.

"I am going to mow my lawn."

Rosie smiled and patted his shoulder. "Of course, it's been neglected for a week, you better make sure it's all right. You know the Meyers hired a service. We could—"

"No way."

"I'm just saying."

He shot her a look, and she shrugged and let it drop. Walter could hardly believe she'd bring it up. Theirs was the nicest lawn on the block, maybe in all of Beaverton. He mulched and seeded and fertilized it all himself. His neighbors had those services come in with their chemicals, and his yard still looked nicer.

"Gonna change." He was turning to walk through the kitchen to the stairway that led up to their bedroom when it struck him that perhaps he could convince his wife to forget his high cholesterol and make her famous egg salad sandwiches for lunch.

He turned and saw Rosie weave a little where she stood and clutch at the coat tree.

"Rose...?" He took a quick step back to her, to catch her, but she waved him off.

"Just got dizzy for a minute." She laughed. "I need some lunch. How about egg salad after you are done with the lawn?"

"You read my mind."

"Coming up." She smiled and Walter turned away, his mind on fertilizer.

WALTER STOOD in the gloom of the garage and considered

his years of junk. The stacks of *Consumer Reports* moldering in the corner, those could go. He'd keep the oak. He was going to make that chest. The old lawn mower, which he liked a lot better than his new one, needed some engine repairs but it was time for him to stop kidding himself. He was never going to get to it.

He wheeled it out to the curb for the garbage guys to take along with the magazines, Jennifer's first bike, and the canoe with the hole. They weren't, as Rosie put it, the camping kind of people, no matter how much he wanted to be.

His father's old fedora sat on the corner of his work-bench. He blew off the thick layer of dust and again, for the millionth time, decided, against his better sense, to keep it.

He wheeled out the new mower that Jennifer and Rosie got him for Christmas, checked the gas and the blades. He pushed it over to the corner of the lawn, pulled the cord, and the hum of the motor blocked out the world. Walter swatted at fly from the lilac bush and decided he'd shake things up a little today.

Today he would mow diagonally.

JENNIFER ATE her sandwich in a hurry and then excused herself to go back to practicing. But he and Rosie lingered, picking at chopped egg yolk and listening to their daughter who, despite her sullen attitude, was growing into a virtu-oso. The only thing she seemed to love was that piano.

"At least she loves something," Rosie said. "I'm so glad something makes her happy."

"She's been pretty good today."

Rosie covered his hand with hers and they listened to Jennifer play warm-up scales that were more complicated and more lovely than anything Walter had ever produced in his life.

"The auditions for the summer program at Columbia are next weekend."

"Chicago? Again? Rosie, we've been over this. I thought we decided no."

"You decided no—stupidly, I might add. This is a huge chance for Jennifer..."

"And a huge expense for us."

"Maybe she'll qualify for a scholarship. We won't know until she tries."

"She'll just get her hopes up, Rosie. What if she doesn't get in? What if she doesn't get a scholarship and we have to tell her no?"

Rosie's breathing was coming fast as she leaned in toward him, and he could not understand why she wanted this so much. Didn't she understand what this could mean for the family? It meant Jennifer might leave and he could not understand how Rosie could be for that.

"You are so scared. Really, Walter. You are the most scared person I know, but I won't let you put your crap on our daughter..."

"I'm not putting my crap on—"

"Yes, you are. You are scared she's going to leave us..."

Sometimes when Rosie nailed him like that, when she proved once again how he had no secrets from her, how she knew him down to his very last thought, he got dizzy from his awe. Dizzy from all that love.

"She's our daughter, Walter. She's not going to leave us."

"Okay, okay, you win. She can audition."

Rosie stood and clapped. "Oh she's going to love this." She ran into the other room and Jennifer's scales stopped, and there was a squeal and some clapping and Walter smiled, hoping that it was the right thing to do, that he hadn't made the biggest mistake of their lives.

The last egg salad sandwich whispered his name.

Rosie came back into the kitchen and stood by his chair to kiss the top of his head. "You made her day."

He nodded and tried to hide the sandwich he shouldn't be eating.

"I'm going to go change," Rosie said. "Maybe take a nap." She walked past him toward the stairs and shot one of those warm looks over her shoulder.

Walter put down the sandwich, wiped his mouth, and followed.

WALTER KNOCKED on his daughter's door and hoped for the best.

"What?" she said through the door.

"Open up, Jen."

He heard the complaining squeak of her mattress and reminded himself that she needed a new one. The door was flung open and his daughter, in all her awkward maturity, glared at him. "What, Dad?"

"You want to go with me to get a video? For after dinner?"

"Right now?"

"Sure."

"I'm busy."

Walter looked behind her and saw nothing but the mess of clothes and music books. "Doing what? Cleaning your room?"

"No."

"So let's go get a video." He tried to keep a smile. He tried to not demand that she go with him, that she change her crappy attitude, that she act happy.

"Dad, I am studying for my auditions next week."

Walter waited for the thank-you. He waited for the acknowledgment that he'd had some sort of effect on her life. But the silence spun out and he, like he always did, got impatient and pissed off with his daughter.

"Fine." He shrugged, feeling like a fool for even trying. He turned and headed back to the kitchen.

"Dad?" Jennifer called out.

"What?"

"If you get *Ghostbusters*," she said. "I'll ask Mom to make some popcorn."

"Carmel corn?"

"Sure."

He nodded, smiling though she couldn't see it. She spoke a totally foreign language, but he knew a *thanks* when he heard one.

THE SUN SET and Rosie sent him outside with a plate of chicken to grill for dinner. He stood out on the small back patio with a can of Coke and watched the world darken. Dogs barked and the smells of the earth changed and he could see fireflies in the purple shadows, blinking and hovering near his freshly cut grass.

The streetlights came on and Jennifer began playing "Yesterday," her newest obsession. It was the twelfth time she'd played it that day, and considering that the eleventh time he'd heard it he wanted to smash the piano, he was surprised that the song seemed right for the moment.

This magic moment of twilight.

"Hey, look." Rosie came out onto the patio and pointed up to the sky.

The moon hung, swollen and ripe, low in the sky and close. Really close. He could see dimples and holes in the surface.

"It does look like cheese."

"Look at all the stars," Rosie whispered, her arm stealing around his waist. "I've never seen so many."

The fathomless black velvet night was shot through with glittering pinpricks. Thousands of them. The sky was a cathedral—majestic and vast. The Milky Way lay strewn carelessly in a thick band across the heavens, like a belt someone dropped.

As they watched, a star fell across the sky, leaving its radiant trail.

"Make a wish," Rosie whispered. She shut her eyes and pressed her lips tight, wishing with all her might like she always did.

Walter looked at his wife and knew there was nothing left to wish for.

"THAT WAS A PRETTY GOOD MOVIE," Rosie said as she brushed out her hair at her dresser.

"You can't beat Bill Murray." Walter shucked off his pants. Shook them out and folded them over the chair. He had the day off tomorrow and was hoping he might get started on repairing the gutters on the garage. They weren't crucial, but another good rain and they'd be in trouble.

"Jennifer loved it."

Walter nodded. He had been struck dumb by the sound of his daughter's unchecked laughter. God, it had been years since she'd been so unguarded around him. They should watch that movie every night.

He eased between the cool sheets and sighed. He crossed his arms behind his head and watched his wife's shoulder's flex and lift as the brush ran through her hair. It turned sable in the low light of the bedside lamp. The strap of her slip slid down her arm and Walter wished Rosie could see herself the way he saw her right now. This moment. She would know there was nothing more winsome.

"What a nice day," Rosie said, and he caught her eye in the mirror.

"It was nice," he sighed. "Come to bed." Rosie smiled and put down the brush. She pulled the blankets free from her side of the bed and slid in next to him.

Immediately she pressed her cold feet to his calves.

"Good God, woman, do you have to do that?"

"It's cold."

"No it's not, it's June."

"Oh," Rosie said, leaning up on her elbow. "I almost forgot. I have a doctor's appointment for a physical tomorrow. Can you take me?"

"Sure, I can take you," Walter said.

The gutters could wait another day.

23

I t seemed to Walter that he blinked and he was in bed with Rosie, and when he blinked again he was alone in a giant king-size bed, Rosie's cold feet no longer pressed to his.

He stared at the ceiling and smiled. What a day. Perfect. The most perfect day there ever was. His joy bubbled and boiled over and he laughed. He had forgotten they had made love that morning. That had been a particularly nice surprise

He sat up and the sheets and thick rose-patterned quilt that were not anything Rosie would have picked out fell from his chest onto his stomach.

He recognized the room. It was the Primrose Suite at the York Hotel in Milwaukee. One year on a business trip, they'd screwed up his regular reservation and he got bumped up to this suite with the king-size bed and the Jacuzzi bathroom and the small sitting room with the fold-out couch.

He stepped out of bed, surprised when his bare feet sank into the thick carpet. He wiggled his toes and nearly giggled.

He felt so young. He patted his stomach but couldn't tell how old he was. There was not a single mirror in the room for him to check. He ran his hand up his neck and his scar was gone.

He felt new.

He pulled open the drapes over the windows. It was sort of rainy, gray, not gloomy, just wet. It was the kind of weather that Rosie liked best. Bath weather, she called it.

There was a low rumble. Walter looked around for the eruption of a filing cabinet through the carpeted floor. But none came.

What in the world?

"Peter? You here?" He looked around for the kid, wondering what he was doing in the Primrose Suite at the York Hotel.

There was a knock on the door. "Room service," a voice said through the mahogany wood, and Walter padded over to open the heavy, ornate door.

Peter, the little shit, in a bell boy uniform, pushed a giant service cart loaded with silver dishes into the room and Walter had to step out of the way or lose a toe.

"Hi Peter," he said with a rush of bonhomie for the guy. "What's going on?"

"Well, we got bacon and some chocolate milkshakes and egg salad sandwiches—"

"What am I doing here?"

"I trust you slept well?" Peter asked, uncovering dishes. Walter knew what the question was. The real question.

"It was everything I wanted it to be," he said. "It was perfect."

"Excellent, glad to hear it," Peter said and then added under his breath, "'Bout damn time."

"But what is this?" Walter gestured to the room, the open

door. "I thought I was out of limbo. I'm ready for what's next." He surprised himself by just how ready he was, eager, even, to fade to black.

"Really?" Peter smirked.

"Yes, I am. I—"

The rumbling noise stopped and Walter turned to stare at the partially open door to the bathroom. The light was on and steam was curling its way around the door.

The noise had been water filling the bath.

"Walter? Is that room service?" It was Rosie's voice coming from behind that cracked door. Water trickled and gurgled, and he knew his wife was in that Jacuzzi bath. "Remember you've got to tip him."

"Yeah, I deserve a heck of a tip," Peter muttered.

"What is this? What—?" Walter could not put words to his hope. If he was wrong...

"It's what you always wanted it to be," Peter told him. "You just needed a little faith."

Walter laughed, but it was more of a sob—he was flooded with things so big he couldn't tell what they were. He turned to Peter, naked and shameless in his relief and joy. But the boy disappeared in a rain of glitter and stardust.

"Walter?" Rosie called. "Where are you?"

"Heaven," he breathed. "I'm in heaven."

DEAR READER - THANK you so much for taking this journey with me. I have been thinking about Walter and Rosie for twenty years and I'm just so thrilled to finally be able to share them with you.

Of course - I'd love it if you felt inclined to leave a review. It would mean a lot.

Also please come find me! Here are the best ways:

Join my newsletter list: http://www.molly-okeefe.com/subscribe/

Follow me on Bookbub: https://www.bookbub.com/profile/2280831212

And Amazon: https://amzn.to/31ZBLWU

Come find me in The Keepers on Facebook: https://www.facebook.com/groups/1657059327869189/

I also have a special treat for you! An EXCLUSIVE excerpt of my next book — Wedding At The Riverview Inn. Available Jan 6. Order HERE

WEDDING At The Riverview Inn

OUT OF THE corner of his eye, Gabe Mitchell saw his father, Patrick, spit a mouthful of seaweed-wrapped tofu into his napkin like a five-year-old.

Gabe kicked him under the table, appalled but envious.

"So?" Melissa, the chef responsible for the vegan spa cuisine, asked. "Was I right, or what?"

"Or what," Patrick muttered, balling his napkin up beside his plate.

"You were right," Gabe said and kept chewing. He chewed and chewed and the bland mouthful didn't break down. He was going to be chewing forever. "This is really something."

"Well?" She smiled broadly. "When do I start?"

Patrick laughed, but quickly coughed to cover it, so Gabe didn't bother kicking him again.

He managed to swallow the bite in his mouth, took a huge sip of the unsweetened berry smoothie to wash it down and was appalled to discover she'd somehow made berries taste bland, too.

He'd interviewed and auditioned five chefs and this one really was the bottom of a very dark, very deep barrel. Not that he had any problem with raw food, or vegan food. It was the food with absolutely no flavor that was really disheartening. It was like she'd taken the flavor *out* of the food.

"Well—" he smiled and lied through his teeth "—I have a few more interviews this week, so I will have to get back to you."

The girl's eagerness turned on a dime and became narrow-eyed mean-spiritedness, which wasn't going to help her get the job. "You know," she said, "it's not going to be easy to find someone willing to live out here in the middle of nowhere."

"I understand that," he said graciously.

"And it's a brand-new inn." She shrugged. "It's not like you have the credentials to get a—"

"Well, then." He stood up and interrupted the defeating diatribe before she got to the part about how he was ugly and his father dressed him funny. "Why don't you gather your equipment and I'll call you if—"

"And that's another thing." Now she was really getting snotty. "Your kitchen is a disaster—"

That one hit him in the gut. Or maybe it was the seaweed finally working it's way through his system but he was suddenly at a loss for words.

"You know how building projects can be." Patrick stood, his silver hair and dashing smile gleaming in the sunlight. "One minute shambles, the next state of the art."

"You must be in the shambles part," Melissa said.

"Very true, but I can guarantee within the week state-of-

the-art." His blue eyes twinkled as though he was letting
Melissa in on a secret. It was times such as these that Gabe
fully realized the compliment people gave him when they
said he was a chip off the old block.

Patrick stepped to the side of Melissa and held out his
arm toward the kitchen as though he were ushering her
toward dinner, rather than away from a job interview she'd
bombed.

Gabe sat with a smile. Dad was going to handle this one.
Great. Because I am out of niceties.

"Tell me, Melissa, how did you get that tofu to stay
together like that? In a tidy little bundle," Patrick asked as
they walked toward the kitchen.

Melissa blushed and launched into a speech on the
magic of toothpicks.

God save me from novice chefs.

The swinging door to the kitchen swung open, revealing
his nowhere-near-completed kitchen, and then swung shut
behind his father giving the terrible chef the heave-ho.

*Gotta hand it to the guy, sixty-seven years old and he still
has it.*

Silence filled the room, from the cathedral ceiling to the
fresh pine wood floors. The table and two chairs sat like an
island in the middle of the vast, sun-splashed room.

He felt as though he was in the eye of the storm. If he
left this room he'd be buffeted, torn apart by gale-force
winds, deadlines, loose ends and a chefless kitchen.

"You're too nice," Patrick said, stepping back into the
room.

"You told me to always be polite," Gabe said.

"Not when you are being poisoned."

Patrick lowered himself into the chair he'd vacated and

crossed his arms over his flannel-covered barrel chest. "She was worse than the other five chefs you've talked to."

The seaweed-wrapped tofu on his plate seemed to mock Gabe, so he threw his napkin over it and pushed it away. At loose ends, he crossed his arms behind his head and stared out his wall of windows at his view of the Hudson River Valley.

The view was stunning. Gorgeous. Greens and grays and clouds like angels filling the slate-blue sky. He banked on that view to bring in the guests to his Riverview Inn, but he'd been hoping for a little more from the kitchen.

The Hudson River snaked its way through the corner of his property, and out the window, he could see the skeleton frame of the elaborate gazebo being built. The elaborate gazebo where, in two and a half months, there was going to be a very important wedding.

The mother of the bride had called out of the blue three days ago, needing an emergency site and had found him on the Web. And she'd been e-mailing every day to talk about the menu and he'd managed to put her off, telling her he needed guest numbers before he could put together a menu and a budget.

If they lost that wedding...well, he'd have to hope there was a manager's job open at McDonald's or that he could sell enough of his blood, or hair, or semen or whatever it took to get him out of the black hole of debt he'd be in.

All of the building was going according to plan. There had been a minor glitch with the plumber, however Max, his brother and begrudging but incredibly skilled general contractor, had sorted it out early and they were right back on track.

"Getting the chef was supposed to be the easy part,

wasn't it?" Patrick asked. "I thought you had those hotshot friends of yours in New York City."

Gabe rolled his eyes at his father. Anyone who didn't know the difference between a fuse box and a circuit breaker was a hotshot to him. And it wasn't a compliment.

"They decided to stay in New York City," he said. All three of his top choices, which had forced him into this hideous interview process.

Fifteen years in the restaurant business working his way up from waiter to bartender to sommelier. He had been the manager of the best restaurant in Albany for four years and finally owner of his own Zagat-rated bar and grill in Manhattan for the past five years and this is what he'd come to.

Flavorless food.

"I can't believe this is so hard," he muttered.

Patrick grinned.

"I open in a month and I've got no chef. No kitchen staff whatsoever."

Patrick chuckled.

"What the hell are you laughing at, Dad? I'm in serious trouble here."

"Your mother would say this—"

Icy anger exploded in his exhausted brain. "What is this recent fascination with Mom? She's been gone for years, I don't care what she'd say."

His cruel words echoed through the empty room. He rubbed his face, weary and ashamed of himself. "I'm sorry, Dad. I've got so much going on, I just don't want—"

"I understand, son." The heavy clap of his father's hand on his shoulder nearly had him crumbling into a heap. "But not everything can be charmed or finessed. Sometimes it takes work—"

"I work." Again, anger rose to the surface. "I work hard, Dad."

"Oh, son." Patrick's voice was rough. "I know you do. But you've worked hard at making it all look easy. I've never seen a construction job go as smooth as this one has. You've got every lawyer, teamster and backhoe operator eating out of the palm of your hand."

"You think that's easy?" Gabe arched an eyebrow at his father.

"I know better than that. I've watched you work that gray in your hair and I've watched you work through the night for this place and I'm proud of you."

Oh, Jesus, he was going to cry in his seaweed. Though at least then it would be salty.

"But sometimes you have to make hard choices. Swallow your pride and beg and compromise and ask for favors. You have to fight, which is something you don't like to do."

That was true, he couldn't actually say he *fought* for things. Fighting implied arguments and standoffs and a possibility of losing.

Losing wasn't really his style.

He worked hard, he made the right contacts, he treated his friends well and his rivals better. He ensured things would go his way—which was a far cry from having them fall in his lap. But it was also a far cry from compromising or swallowing his pride or fighting.

The very idea gave Gabe the chills.

"You saying I should fight for Melissa?" He jerked his head at the door the vchef had left through.

"No." Patrick's bushy eyebrows lifted. "God, no. But I'm saying you should fight for the right chef."

"What're we fighting for?" Max, Gabe's older brother stomped into the room, brushing sawdust from the chest and arms of his navy fleece onto the floor. "Did I miss lunch?"

"Not really," Patrick said. "And we haven't actually started any fight, so cool your jets."

Max pulled one of the chairs from the stacks on tables in the corner, unclipped his tool belt and slung it over the back of the chair before sitting.

As the family expert on fighting, Max had made battles his life mission. And not just physically, though the bend in his nose attested to a few bar brawls and the scar on his neck from a bullet that got too close told the truth better than this new version of his brother, who, since being shot, acted as though he'd never relished a good confrontation.

Yep, Max knew how to fight, for all the good it did him.

"Well, from the look on Gabe's face, I guess we still don't have a chef," Max said, sliding his sunglasses into the neck of his shirt.

"No," Gabe growled. "We don't."

Now Max, his beloved brother, his best friend, stretched his arms over his head and laughed. "Never seen you have so much trouble, Gabe."

"I am so glad that my whole family is getting such pleasure out of this. Need I remind you that if this doesn't work, we're all homeless. You should show a little concern about what's going on."

"It's just a building," Max said.

Gabe couldn't agree less, but he kept his mouth shut. Going toe to toe with his brother, while satisfying on so many levels, wouldn't get him a chef.

"I'm going to go make us some lunch." Patrick stood and Max groaned. "Keep complaining and you can do it," he said over his shoulder and disappeared into the kitchen.

"Cheese sandwiches. Again," Max groused.

"It's better than what we had, trust me."

"What happened?"

"Ah, she fed us terrible food and then said I was crazy for trying to build an inn in the middle of nowhere and get a chef to come out here for little pay in a half-finished kitchen. Basically, what all the chefs have said to me."

Gabe paused, then gathered the courage to ask the question that had been keeping him up nights.

"Do you think they're right? Is it nuts to expect a high-caliber chef to come way out here and put their career on the line and their life on hold to see if this place takes off?"

Max tipped his head back and howled, the sound reverberating through the room, echoing off the vaulted ceiling. "Brother, I've been telling you this was nuts for over a year. Don't tell me you're starting to agree now!"

Gabe smiled. He was discouraged, sure. Tired as all hell, without a doubt. Frustrated and getting close to psychotic about his chefless state, absolutely. But his Riverview Inn was going to be a success.

He'd work himself into the hospital, into his grave to make sure of it.

He had been dreaming of this inn for ten years.

"It's not like I've got no credentials." He scowled, hating that Melissa had gotten under his skin and that he still felt the need to justify his dream. "I worked my way up to manager in the restaurant in Albany. And I owned one of the top ten restaurants in New York City for five years. I've had reporters and writers calling me for months wanting to do interviews. The restaurant reviewer for *Bon Appetit* wanted to come out and see the property before we even got started."

"All the more reason to get yourself a great chef."

"Who?" He rubbed his hands over his face.

"Call Alice," Max said matter-of-factly, as though Alice was on speed dial or something.

Gabe's heart chugged and sputtered.

He couldn't breathe for a minute. It'd been so long since someone had said her name out loud. *Alice.*

"Who?" he asked through a dry throat. Gabe knew, of course. How many Alices could one guy know? But, surely his brother, his best friend, had not pulled *Alice* from the past and suggested she was the solution to his problems.

"Don't be stupid." Max slapped him on the back. "The whole idea of this place started with her—"

"No, it didn't." Gabe felt compelled to resist the whole suggestion. *Alice* had never, ever been the solution to a problem. She was the genesis of trouble, the spring from which any disaster in his life emerged.

Max shook his head and Gabe noticed the silver in his brother's temples had spread to pepper his whole head and sprouted in his dark beard. This place was aging them both. "We open in a month and you want to act like a five-year-old?" Max asked.

"No, of course not. But my ex-wife isn't going to help things here."

"She's an amazing chef." Max licked his lips. "I can't tell you the number of times I've woken up in a cold sweat thinking of that duck thing she made with the cherries."

Gabe worried at the cut along his thumb with his other thumb and tried not to remember all the times in the past five years he'd woken in a cold sweat thinking of Alice.

"Gabe." Max laid a hand on Gabe's shoulder. "Be smart."

"Last I heard she was a superstar," Gabe said. He tried to relax the muscles of his back, his arms that had gone tight at the mention of Alice. He tried to calm his heart. "She wouldn't be interested."

"When was the last you heard?"

It's not as though she'd stayed in touch after that first year when they'd divvied up all the things they'd gathered and collected—the antiques from upstate, their kitchen, their friends. "About four years ago."

"Well, maybe she'll know of someone. She can at least point you in the right direction."

Gabe groaned. "I hate it when you're right," he muttered.

"Well, I'd think you'd be used to it by now." Max laughed. "I think I'll skip lunch and get back to work." He grabbed his tool belt. "The gazebo should be done by tomorrow."

"What's the status on the cottages?" Gabe asked.

"You'll have to ask Dad." Max shrugged his broad shoulders and cinched the tool belt around his waist, over his faded and torn jeans. "As far as I know he just had some roofing and a little electrical to finish on the last one."

Gabe's affection and gratitude toward his brother and dad caught him right in the throat. The Riverview Inn with its cottages, stone-and-beam lodge and gazebo and walking trails and gardens had been his dream, the goal of his entire working life. But he never, ever would have been able to accomplish it without his family.

"Max, I know I don't say it enough, but thank you. I—"

Max predictably held up a hand. "You can thank me by providing me with some decent chow. It's not too much to ask."

He took his sunglasses from the neck of his fleece and slid them on, looking dangerous, like the cop he'd been and not at all like the brother Gabe knew.

"Oh, I almost forgot," Max said, poised to leave. "Sheriff Ginley has got two more kids."

"Can either of them cook?"

Max shrugged. "I think one of them got fired from McDonald's."

"Great, he can be our chef."

"I don't think Sheriff Ginley would smile upon a juvenile delinquent with such easy access to knives."

The after-school work program for kids who got in trouble in Athens, the small town north of the inn, had been Max's idea, but Gabe had to admit, the labor was handy, and he hoped they were doing some good for the kids. "They can help you with the grounds."

"That's what I figured." Max smiled wickedly and left, his heavy-booted footsteps thudding through the nearly empty room.

Gabe sighed and let his head fall back. He stared up at the elaborate cedar joists in the ceiling, imagined them with the delicate white Christmas lights he planned on winding around them.

The ceiling would look like the night sky dotted with stars.

It had been one of Alice's ideas.

He and Alice used to talk about opening a place out of the city. A place on a bluff. He'd talked about cottages and fireplaces and she'd talked about organic ingredients and local produce. They'd been a team then, she the chef, he the consummate host, producer and manager. He'd felt invincible in those early days with Alice by his side.

But then the problems came and Alice got more and more distant, more and more sad with every trip to the doctor, every failed effort that ended in blood and tears and —Well, he'd never felt so helpless in his life.

"Lunch, boys!" Dad called from the kitchen the way he had since their mom walked out on them more than thirty years ago.

Gabe smiled and stood.

Nothing to do but eat a cheese sandwich and get to work. His dream wasn't going to build itself.

~

The hangover pounded behind Alice's eyes. Her fingers shook, so she set down the knife before she diced up her finger along with the tomatoes.

"I'm taking a break," she told Trudy, who worked across from her at the long stainless steel prep table.

Trudy's black eyes were concerned. "That's your second break since you've been here and it's only three."

"Smoker's rights," Alice croaked and grabbed a mug from the drying rack by the industrial washer and filled it with the swill Johnny O's called coffee.

"You don't smoke," Trudy pointed out, trying to be helpful and failing miserably. "If Darnell comes back here, what am I supposed to tell him?"

"That he can fire me." Alice slid her sunglasses from her coat hanging by the door and used her hips to push out into the bright afternoon.

Even with her dark glasses on, the sunshine felt like razor wire against her eyeballs, so after she collapsed onto the bench that had been set up by the dumpsters for staff, she just shut her eyes against the sun.

The hangover, the sleeplessness, this mindless menial job that paid her part of the mortgage, it all weighed her down like sandbags attached to her neck.

Tonight no drinking, she swore.

She couldn't change the fact that she'd fallen from chef

and owner of Zinnia's to head line chef at one of the three Johnny O's franchises in Albany. That damage was already done and she'd come to grips with it.

But she could control the drinking.

A small voice reminded her that she made that promise almost every night.

Sometimes she wanted to punch the small voice, but instead she breathed deep of the slightly putrid air and tried to get Zen about the whole situation. She took a sip of her coffee, and listened to the sound of traffic.

The parking lot was pretty empty, but soon the hungry folks of Albany would be getting off work and looking for a sunny patio and drink specials and a lot of them would head to Johnny O's. The kitchen would be loud and on fire for about eight hours and in those eight hours, while arranging plates of pasta and fire-baked pizzas and grilling steaks and fish specials, she would forget all the reasons she had to drink.

Maybe she'd help the cleaning staff tonight. Work herself into a good exhaustion so she wouldn't need the red wine to relax.

She tilted her face up to the sun and stretched out her feet, pleased with her plan.

A black truck, mud splattered and beat-up, pulled in to the lot and parked directly across from her. She thought about heading back inside, or at least opening the door and yelling to warn Trudy customers were arriving and the kitchen was on demand. But Trudy had been in the business as long as she had and could handle cooking for a truckload of guys.

But only one guy got out.

One guy, holding a droopy bouquet of yellow roses.

One guy, whose slow amble toward her was painfully, heartbreakingly familiar.

Coffee sloshed onto her pants, so she set the cup down on the bench and clenched her suddenly shaking hands together.

Spots swam in front of her eyes and her head felt light and full, like a balloon about to pop.

The man was tall and lean, so handsome still it made her heart hurt.

He stopped right in front of her and pushed his sunglasses up onto his head, displacing his dark blond hair. The sun was behind him and he seemed so big. She used to love his size, love how it made her feel small and safe. He'd wrap those strong arms around her and she felt protected from the world, from herself.

He smiled like a man who knew all the tastiest things about her.

That smile was his trademark. He could disarm an angry patron at four feet with the strength of his charming smile. He could woo frigid reviewers, disgruntled suppliers...his ex-wife.

"Hello, Alice." He held out the roses but she couldn't get her hands to lift and take them.

She left her shades on, so shattered by Gabe's sudden appearance in front of her, as if the past five years hadn't happened.

"Gabe." Her voice croaked again and she nearly cringed.

He took a deep breath, in through his nose, no doubt hoping for a bit more welcome from her, some reaction other than the stoic front that was all she had these days.

His hand holding the roses fell back to his side.

"What are you doing here?" she asked. She sounded

accusatory and mean, like a stranger who had never known him at all.

And she felt that way. It was why, in part, the marriage had ended. Despite the late-night talks, the dreams of building a business together, the sex that held them together longer than they should have been, in the end, when things got bad, they really never knew each other at all.

"I could ask you the same thing." His eyes swept the bench, the back door to Johnny O's. The Dumpsters.

Suddenly, the reality of her life hammered home like a nail in her coffin. She worked shifts at a chain restaurant and was hungover at three on a Friday afternoon.

Oh, how the mighty have fallen, she thought bitterly, hating herself with a vehemence she usually saved for her dark drunken hours.

"I work here," she said, battling her embarrassment with the sharp tilt of her head.

He nodded and watched her, his blue eyes cataloging the differences the five years between them had made. And behind her sunglasses, she did the same.

Gabe Mitchell was still devilishly easy on the eyes.

He'd always had her number. One sideways look from him, one tiny grin and she'd trip over her hormones to get into his arms. There was just something about the man and, she surmised after taking in his faded jeans and the black T-shirt with the rip at the collar, the work boots and his general all-around sexiness, there still was something about him.

But, she reminded herself, underneath that lovely candy coating beat one cold, cold heart. She'd learned it the hard way, and she still hadn't recovered from the frost burn her five-year marriage had given her.

Call it fear of commitment, call it intimacy issues, whatever it was, Gabe had it bad. And watching him walk away from her and their marriage had nearly killed her.

"You look good," Gabe said and it was such a lie, such an attempt to sweet-talk her, that she laughed. "You do," he protested.

"Save the charm for someone else, Gabe." Finally she pushed her shades up onto her head and looked her ex-husband in the eye. "I told you I never wanted to see you again."

Preorder now!

AFTERWORD

This story has been with me for over ten years. One morning after the birth of our son I asked my husband which day he would rather relive - our wedding or the birth of our son.

I thought, frankly, he'd say our wedding. Because it was a good party and that sweet man loves a party.

And he said neither. He'd want a quiet day. A trip to the park with our son in the stroller. Our dog catching tennis balls. A good meal. A visit with friends. But it was tricky because those days were never particularly memorable. They blended together and without some event, it would be impossible to pick a day.

Unless it was your last quiet simple day.

That's how Walter came to be.

Printed in Poland
by Amazon Fulfillment
Poland Sp. z o.o., Wrocław

53887850R00134